Children of the Crystal Vision

Father Lee Kaylor
with
Patricia Kaylor

Irisa Publishing

Copyright © 2001 by Father Lee Kaylor, Patricia Kaylor

Library of Congress Catalog Card Number: 2001 132587
ISBN: 0-9672695-1-2
First Edition

Published by Irisa Publishing
              Sonoma, California

Manufactured in the United States of America

ABOUT THE AUTHORS

Father Lee Kaylor was ordained for the Archdiocese of San Francisco in 1981. He has a Master's degree from St. Patrick's Seminary in Menlo Park, California and a Bachelor's degree in Anthropology from Kent State University.

He became a chaplain in the United States Air Force and served in Saudi Arabia and Kuwait at the end of Operation Desert Storm.

At the time of the bombing of the Alfred P. Murrah Building, he was stationed at Tinker Air Force Base in Oklahoma City, and assisted in the rescue effort along with Air Force personnel.

Father Kaylor founded Priests For Life, an international association of Catholic pro-life clergy, in 1990.

*   *   *   *   *

Patricia Kaylor is the mother of six children, of whom Father Lee Kaylor is the eldest.

She was invited by John Cardinal O'Connor of New York to be one of the seven founding sisters of the new order of "The Sisters of Life."

She now resides in Oklahoma on the family ranch where she is planning a new book.

DEDICATION

To Vicki Evans

Without whom this book

would never have seen

the light of day.

St. Michael the Archangel, defend us in battle.

Be our protection against the wickedness and snares of the devil.

May God rebuke him, we humbly pray.

And do thou, O Prince of the heavenly host, by the power of God, cast into hell Satan and all the evil spirits who roam through the world seeking the ruin of souls.

Prayer to St. Michael the Archangel

PROLOGUE

A breeze coming off the sea blew through the open window across from Janet's desk ruffling her dark brown hair and tossing the papers she was grading to the floor. She raised her head and inhaled deeply, savoring the aroma of the sea.

Janet loved the sea and everything about it including the smell of dying seaweed. It was a beautiful autumn day and the temptation to go outside to stroll through the village down to the beach tugged at her but she pulled herself back to the papers that needed to be graded.

Janet Wayland doubled as English teacher and senior counselor. It was a full load, but she loved her work and the students knew it. She was the most popular teacher at Valley High School and she felt it was important that she be available to her students whenever she was not in her classroom.

The final bell rang just as she knelt to pick up the papers. A shy tapping on the open door brought a quick smile to the counselor's face. One of her favorite students stood in the doorway.

"Miss Wayland, may I come in? I really need to talk to you if you're not too busy."

"Of course, Shelby, I always have time to talk. That's what I'm here for."

The girl knelt down to help retrieve the scattered pages.

"What is it, Shelby? You seem so troubled. Please, sit down. Tell me what's bothering you. I'd like to help if I can."

"Oh, Miss Wayland, I don't know how to start."

"Well, the best place to start is at the beginning. I have all the time we need."

Tears began to slowly wind down the pretty girl's face. Janet handed her a box of tissues and gave her time to collect her thoughts. Janet tried to calm the girl down with a change in conversation.

"Are you still working in the dining room at the Country Club?"

"Yes, Miss Wayland," she sobbed.

"I'm sure your parents must be very proud of you. I imagine they could easily afford to pay for your college expenses."

"Yes, they would have, but I wanted to do what I could myself."

"I think that's a great attitude. Would you like to tell me what's bothering you?"

"I don't know where to begin." Tears began to flow as she reached for more tissues. "I'm so scared and I'm afraid to tell my parents."

"Would this have anything to do with your boyfriend? Are you pregnant, Shelby?"

"Oh, no, Miss Wayland. I'm not pregnant. But, yes, it does concern my boyfriend and some of my friends."

Janet leaned forward and took the girl's hand. Shelby grabbed her hand and clung to it as though it were a lifeline thrown to a drowning man. Words began to pour out of the frightened girl in a flood of tears.

****

Sunset found Janet Wayland sitting on a large boulder that jutted out into the sea. She passed the time by counting the waves as they slapped up against her perch. Every thirteenth wave, much higher than the previous twelve, would come crashing into her rock, spraying her with salt water.

There were no stars out tonight, and the moon kept disappearing behind dark and drifting clouds creating a black mirror-like finish to the ocean. Yet the ocean was anything but quiet as the waves roared and crashed against the large rocks that lay in their path as they raced to the shifting beach.

The rhythmic surging of the sea lost its hypnotic grip on her senses when a large wave broke noisily upon her rocky sanctuary. The fine salt mist tingled in her nostrils clearing her head like a bracing slap.

Roused as from a trance, she gradually became conscious of a muffled silence that seemed to envelop her. The fog was beginning to move in off the water, sliding smoothly and silently across the shiny surface like an enormous white wall.

It reminded her of a looming iceberg. A half hour ago, the fog bank had seemed far away. A distant threat upon the horizon. Soft and warm, it now blanketed the shore and crept along the road behind her.

Janet was surprised to see how fast it had come. And although she sat not a hundred yards from busy Highway One, the fog had completely erased the traffic from her view, as well as muted the sounds from the well-traveled road.

Janet had always loved this particular spot, in spite of its reputation. It had been nicknamed Mortuary Beach by the natives because there had been so many drowning accidents along this stretch of Pacific Coast. Its proper name listed on the maps was Monastery Beach because it sat just below the old Benedictine Monastery nestled high on the hillside behind her.

No one familiar with this beach and the fierce undertow would ever think of swimming these waters. The beach was rarely visited, and the solitude was one reason Janet loved to sit here, staring out over the ocean. On a clear evening, she would watch the ships as they sailed south from San Francisco.

The pretty brunette's thoughts drifted back to the conversation she'd had with Shelby earlier that afternoon. She knew how vulnerable teens could be, even the ones like Shelby, who came from good, stable, loving families.

Their search for an independent identity and their unshakable belief in their own invulnerability could take them down some pretty perilous roads. From the ridiculous to the tragic, she had seen where all that experimenting could lead. Her own youth wasn't so far gone that she couldn't feel a familiar pang at recalling some of her youthful indiscretions. She had heard and seen a lot but nothing like what she had heard a few hours ago in her office.

Janet's nerves were still strained from the emotionally charged encounter with the terrified girl. As she recounted the elements of Shelby's tale, she had to admit that it sounded bizarre.

A lone gull shrieked overhead searching for prey. The sudden high-pitched cry raked across Janet's nerves like fingernails across a blackboard. She had promised to help Shelby, but how? A meeting with Shelby's parents? The school administration? Or perhaps even the police?

The bells from the monastery began to toll calling the nuns to vespers. Even though the monastery stood just across the highway, the bells sounded muffled and strangely distant. How perfectly Gothic, Janet thought as the echo reverberated through the haze.

If only it were another time. Back in the Middle Ages they had easier answers to complex questions, and simpler more direct methods of dealing with things.

She smiled, thinking of how the good sisters across the highway might react to Shelby's story. "Ring the bell, close the book, quench the candle", she intoned in mock seriousness reciting the ancient formula for excommunication.

But the devil seemed to have gone out of fashion these days, even in the Church. In truth, she really wasn't sure how the sisters would react. Despite the Hollywood cliches that even she loved to cling to, she had found the Benedictine nuns to be a surprisingly sophisticated collection of women. Janet's familiarity with the monastery sprang from the field trips she had taken her students on over the past couple of years.

The building was on the historic register and had become an object of secular pilgrimages for artists, historians and architects. A high-school tour of the monastery's gardens, chapel and museum always ended in the speak-room and a visit with the prioress, Mother Benedicta.

To Janet she seemed as unlike those stern disciplinarians who had taught her in Catholic grammar school as anyone could possibly be. Time and again the canny old nun had proven more than a match for the somewhat jaded youth who stared at her in bug-eyed wonderment from the opposite side of the grille.

With humor and transparent sincerity, she maneuvered her way through interrogations that would have made a sailor blush. Held enthralled by smiling eyes, the offspring of the rich and powerful listened to stories of a life of poverty, chastity and obedience. Janet wished she could look into those eyes now.

Janet became abruptly aware that she was no longer alone on the beach. The mesmerizing pattern of the waves and the droning of the surf had lulled her into a dreamy calm, which was shattered by the feeling that she was being watched. She felt the hairs on the back of her neck begin to bristle.

Janet sensed, more than heard, a presence gathering behind her and she was suddenly afraid to turn around. Fear, like a cold hand, began to clutch at her until it became an almost physical sensation. The chill of terror that crawled over her was like being enveloped in clammy strands of seaweed.

The sound of footsteps crunching on the wet sand behind her hit her consciousness like a punch to the stomach, leaving her breathless and faint.

Through sheer force of will, Janet turned her head toward the sound coming from the beach behind her. Something was moving in the swirling mist. She strained to make out the strange form advancing toward her.

"What in God's name?" she whispered, the words catching in her throat. It appeared to move like some impossible snake, undulating in a serpentine path toward her.

As the shape emerged from the creeping fog, its true nature came clearly into focus. It wasn't one creature at all, but a single file line of shadowy figures in long tattered, flowing robes that billowed about them, creating the illusion of a single entity.

They came to a halt in the dunes above, standing like statues. There was something menacing and evil about the way the silhouettes just stood there, staring down at her.

Janet's heart pounded in her chest like a bird flapping against its cage trying to escape. She strained to keep her eyes focused as waves of vapor swirled over the apparition.

She began to panic as she heard her name being called out of the fog..."Janet...Janet." Like a curtain pulled back, the billowing mist parted for an instant and she could see that there were others gathered on the dunes.

In a fog-muffled chant they, too, began to take up the chorus, "Janet...Janet...Janet". All at once, almost as a single entity, they began to descend to the beach, never looking away from her.

For an instant, she tore her eyes away from them and quickly scanned the beach, searching for a way to flee. There was nowhere to run. They had cut off her escape.

Gripped by fear, she was unable to move, her legs welded to the cold stone. A rush of adrenaline snapped the chains of her inertia and she lurched forward. She seemed to move in slow motion, as if in a nightmare.

Her foot came down unevenly and she knew in a horrifying second that it was too late.

Trying to regain her balance on the slippery rock, she reached out, arms flailing, but there was nothing to grasp onto but thin air.

The last thing Janet saw as she plunged backward into the cold, black sea were the ghostly phantoms rushing toward her out of the gray mist.

Black water closed over her head as she plummeted down. The undertow pulled at her with icy fingers.

Her lungs burned as she fought for air, fighting not to suck in the freezing water. She called up every bit of strength in her body to pull herself free.

Just as her head broke the surface, the thirteenth wave picked her up like a rag doll and smashed her into the jagged rocks.

For an instant, her body was ablaze in blinding pain. The world around her faded away into blackness.

Chapter 1

It was only one hundred twenty miles from San Francisco to the village of Carmel-by-the-Sea. Two hours if one wasn't too scrupulous about the speed limit.

Father Mark Ross glanced in the rear-view mirror to make sure the coast was clear. He had heard a lot of confessions in the eight years he had been a priest, but he had never heard anyone confess to breaking the speed limit.

The image of Cornelius Walsh, S.J. flashed across his mind. (S.J. being the initials for "Society of Jesus," the official name of the Jesuit Order.) Even now, more than a decade later, the memory of his mentor's labyrinthine, hair-splitting classroom dissertations on the immoral versus the merely illegal brought an amused smile to his face.

He could still hear his classmate, Bucky Harrigan, leaning over to whisper, "New and deep meaning to the word 'Jesuitical'."

The Jesuits did seem to play by a different set of rules. Father Ross could remember the first joke he'd heard upon arriving at St. Anselm's Seminary. A Franciscan, a Dominican and a Jesuit were debating the various merits of their illustrious orders and arguing about which one God favored the most. They decided to settle the question by taking it to the top.

They agreed to write the question on a piece of paper to leave it on the high altar overnight and return in the morning for the answer. The next day, they read the Most High's reply. "My dear children, I love you all equally. Signed, God, S.J."

The traffic was light, and Father Ross enjoyed being just a little ahead of the pack with a clear field of vision opening up before him. But reckless was not a word that one would associate with him. Besides, he was not unaware of the unspoken gentlemen's agreement between the average motorist and the California Highway Patrol. A polite five miles over the speed limit would be tolerated, but not one mile more.

As he pressed the accelerator of the new emerald green Dodge Neon, the engine hummed in an easy and unlabored way that brought back a glimmer of the satisfaction he had often felt over the past few weeks since the purchase of his first new car. No "buyer's remorse" here.

At six feet, four inches tall, the priest often amazed and amused his friends and parishioners when they saw him emerge from a sub-compact car.

"Hey, Father, hold on a second while I get my can opener," Tony Malatesa, the parish custodian, had said when he saw Mark extricate himself for the first time. Mark's enthusiasm was undimmed.

As far as he was concerned, there was more than enough room for the driver and, to date, his sole passenger, the priest's constant companion, a jet black Scottish Terrier named Angus.

The canine was true to his breed. A one-man dog who loved nothing more than to be with his master. Anywhere Ross went was fine with Angus, as long as he went too.

Whether resting his head on the priest's foot like a pillow while he prepared his homilies or stationed under his desk like a protecting sphinx while he counseled newlyweds, Angus was Mark Ross's black shadow.

Sitting next to his master on the front seat with his paws on the dash, the terrier struggled valiantly to maintain the dignity of his upright position as the car took the twists and turns of Highway 17, winding its way past Los Gatos and up through the Santa Cruz mountains.

Mark loved this part of California more than any place on earth. The dramatic contrasts seemed to open his soul. The Coast Range rose up as a natural barrier between the populous cities of northern California's Bay area---San Francisco, Oakland, San Jose---and the casual, quiet towns of the central coast.

The four-lane Santa Cruz highway ascends rapidly through steep green slopes of ancient redwood forests like a giant escalator lifting you up and out of the Bay-area smog. Some of these giant trees were two thousand years old and almost three hundred feet high.

In mist-shrouded ravines, stands of primeval redwoods crowded so thickly that parts of the forest hadn't seen the full light of day since Columbus was yet a name unknown. These silent sentinels had witnessed much and kept their secrets.

After the "Summer of Love" imploded in the aftermath of Charles Manson, and the fighting in Vietnam ended, refugees from the Haight-Ashbury drifted south in a psychedelic haze to "drop out" on the golden beaches of Santa Cruz while the rest of the world moved on.

Graying flower children, a little wilted now, abounded along the central coast. Mark Ross had seen them often in their tie-dyed bell bottoms and love beads, singing Dylan tunes for spare change and driving ancient Volkeswagon vans up and down the Pacific Coast Highway on an endless odyssey still in search of the Age of Aquarius.

The ones to be pitied were the children of these latter-day lotus eaters, the ones with vacant expressions and names like "Sunflower", "Moonbeam" and "Tamalpais". They seemed to represent some Sixties counter-culture version of the Amish people frozen in a particular place and time that existed for no one else but themselves.

There were other denizens who lived in these Santa Cruz mountains. On a regular basis, abandoned cars would be found along the side of Highway 17. Emergency flashers blinking, hood propped open, AAA sunvisors placed against the windshield, silently pleading for assistance, but empty.

For a couple of weeks the television stations would broadcast pictures of the vanished travelers together with tearful pleas for information from anguished relatives. But no one was ever found. And then it would happen that six months or a year later a family dog in nearby Los Gatos or Scott's Valley would come in from the woods one day carrying a human femur in its mouth and proudly drop it at the feet of its horrified master.

The grisley chain of thought cast a momentary, melancholy shadow over the radiant October afternoon. He snapped back to reality as he nearly careened into a concrete lane divider while negotiating a particularly sharp curve. Scottish determination proved no match for centrifugal force and Angus tumbled off the seat to the floor.

Dazed, but quickly recovering his dignity, he jumped back onto the front seat, and planted his paws firmly on the dash with a noise peculiar to Scotties that left no doubt as to his opinion of Ross's driving skills.

"Sorry, Fuzz Face," Ross said, running his hand over the dog's wiry coat. "Festina Lente---make haste slowly, as they used to say in the seminary, right? Carmel isn't going anywhere. It will be waiting for us when we get there."

Angus cocked his head to one side and stared intently at Mark, in that canine manner with which every dog lover was familiar, giving the impression that the terrier was straining with every fiber to understand him.

Mark cocked his own head to one side, mimicking the dog's quizzical expression. Angus responded with an excited huffing noise. Mark continued to scratch the dog's ears until Angus turned his head to examine something of particular interest that flashed along the passenger's side window.

Normally Angus would never be the first to walk away from a back rub. In fact, the look of bliss on the terrier's face whenever Mark scratched his ears reminded him of those levitating saints in ecstasy pictured in those sentimental holy cards he remembered from his youth.

He wondered if dogs were capable of altered states of consciousness. But in the hierarchy of fun and excitement, nothing topped a car ride. It seemed to Mark that dogs needed the mental stimulation of new sights and sounds and smells as much as people did.

Mark was ready for the stimulation of new vistas himself. He was eager to begin his vacation---a month of sun, sand and blessed silence. There would be no doorbells or telephones ringing at all hours. No hospital emergencies in the middle of the night. No battling couples whose marriages were already fractured beyond repair. No surly teen-agers being dragged to the rectory by their mothers to be "straightened out by Father" because they had been caught with a Playboy magazine or a quarter of an ounce of oregano that they thought was pot. Only the rhythmic pounding of the waves and the occasional sound of the bells calling the nuns to prayer.

Mark had been coming to the cloistered Benedictine monastery in Carmel for seven years. He was part of a succession of priests who served as substitute chaplains for the sisters when their regular chaplain, Father Denis LeMoine, was taking his vacation---usually six months in Paris.

It was hard to imagine how anyone could ever become tired of Carmel and the Monterey Peninsula, but Denis did. Now in his early sixties, he had come to the monastery at the age of thirty-eight to die. Diagnosed with cancer while working as a priest in nearby Monterey, the monastery seemed like a quiet, serene place where Father Denis could spend his last earthly days surrounded by the exquisite beauty of Carmel and the holy ministrations of the Sisters.

It would have made a peaceful death. But by now, Denis had outlived two bishops, a Mother Superior and a good many of his contemporaries. In a word, he had rallied. And rallied with a joie de vivre that made him the toast of the exclusive Pebble Beach crowd. His name was a household word in the mansions along the Seventeen Mile Drive.

Denis had a witty sophistication and Gallic good looks that made him a perennial on all the best guest lists, a raconteur who could shoot his own age in a golf game at Pebble Beach.

Denis personally knew every maitre d' in the finest restaurants between San Francisco and San Luis Obispo. It was said that the most difficult decision he had to face each day was deciding which dinner invitation to accept that evening.

Denis was also a very effective and much-loved priest. He could inspire in wealthy dowagers and the retired captains of industry a love for God and an interest in their fellow man that they did not know they had. He could involve them in projects to which, without his friendship and influence, they would never have given a second thought.

Among his accomplishments was a mission he had founded with the help of his wealthy patrons to care for the spiritual and material needs of the migrant farm workers who came to pick the fertile fields of Salinas and Monterey.

He loved the nuns and the nuns loved him. But they were just as happy as he was each year when his vacation time arrived. They enjoyed the diversity and energy of the young priests who would come for month-long intervals in his absence. Father Mark Ross was one of their favorites, which is why they kept inviting him back year after year.

It was early afternoon when Mark slid down the sunset slopes of the Santa Cruz Mountains towards the western sea. Connecting with the Pacific Coast Highway in Santa Cruz, he swung south toward the Monterey Peninsula. There were shorter routes but this was his favorite. The coast highway took him along the clustered time shares and beach-front condominiums that made up most of Rio del Mar and La Selva Beach, past long stretches of gently rolling pine, and on toward the sand dunes of Fort Ord.

He knew that once they reached the Fort, Monterey would almost be in sight. Then it was only a quick climb over the crest of the peninsula and down to the village of Carmel-by-the-Sea.

The Monterey peninsula is a square piece of California coastline that juts out into the Pacific about one hundred miles south of San Francisco. On the north side of the peninsula lies the scenic town of Monterey, with its picturesque bay and romantic history.

The red-tiled roofs and white adobe walls of its restored old town quarter conjured up for Mark images of dashing caballeros, raven-haired senoritas flirting behind lace fans, and the sound of mission bells when California was the jewel of Spain's colonial empire.

Across town, "Cannery Row," made famous in John Steinbeck's novels as home to bordellos, honkytonks and Bohemians, is now the site of expensive hotels, overpriced restaurants, yuppie watering holes and souvenir shops.

On the seaward side of the peninsula lie the two tiny communities of Pacific Grove and Pebble Beach. The former, famous for the annual migration of the Monarch Butterflies that vacation there on their sojourn to South America, and the latter, which is basically a golf course surrounded by an exclusive retirement community.

Nestled along the southern side of the peninsula is the village of Carmel. And blanketing it all is the lush green cypress and pine canopy of the Del Monte Forest.

As they cleared the dunes south of Fort Ord, Angus began to shift from foot to foot and stood up against the dashboard with a long growl.

"Hang on, Angus, we're almost there," Mark said trying to calm the nervous dog. As they crested the top of a hill, the priest became aware of what was troubling his companion---the sky had changed ominously. It seemed as if the whole Monterey peninsula had been plunged into the twilight of a total eclipse.

It was the middle of the afternoon, but the sun had disappeared from the sky. The normally translucent blue-greens of the bay and the brilliant orange California Poppies growing amid the dunes along the highway seemed suddenly drained of color. The riotous hues of the central coast seemed to melt together into a dull and lifeless gray. It was unnatural, apocalyptic.

As the priest drove deeper into the eerie twilight, the acrid stench of smoke began to assail his nostrils--- fire…and it was close.

Californians had grown accustomed to fires. Thousands of acres were lost every year. And when the Santa Ana winds swept in from the south, Mother Nature could create an unstoppable blowtorch the size of Rhode Island, consuming everything in its path. By any standards, this one had to be a monster.

Reaching for the radio, he began to scan for a station that might have some information about the conflagration. He didn't relish the prospect of turning a corner and finding himself at the Gates of Hell.

Chapter 2

As Mark turned into the drive and looked up at the monastery, he could barely recognize the building through the smoke. There was a heavy brown haze swirling around the white marble bell tower. He slowed the car down and stared at what looked like a vision of a Moorish castle floating in mid-air.

Set into the side of what was usually an emerald green hillside, the monastery was a favorite subject for local artists and photographers. The building itself was a long, two-storied, white-washed rectangle with turrets and towers and burnt-orange clay tile roofs.

Its second-story windows looked out to one of the most stunning views on the Pacific Coast. Framed by a stretch of the most beautiful coastline in the world, it found its way into innumerable tourist brochures, photo journals and coffee-table books.

Like a forbidding palisade, California's Santa Lucia Range runs right up against the shores of the Pacific. In many places there is little more than the Pacific Coast Highway and a narrow strip of beach between the foaming waves of the ocean and this colossal serpentine wall that plunges down steeply to the sea.

To the south was Point Lobos, with its moss-veiled cypress groves and its deep, endlessly churning aquamarine coves. Facing the monastery was Monastery Beach, well known to the locals for its treacherous riptides and unpredictable waves which claimed the life of more than one heedless soul lured by its deceptively peaceful disguise.

And to the north, lay the artist colony of Carmel-by-the-Sea, an easy three-mile walk through the dunes. From the low-lying cliffs above Monastery Beach, the eighteenth century Spanish Mission of San Carlos Borromeo could be seen dozing alongside the marshy Carmel River. On a particularly ambitious day, the river might actually make it across the sand dunes all the way to the ocean.

Most of the time, however, it just lazed around in the warm California sunshine, too relaxed and cozy right where it was to be bothered about going on any farther.

The incredible beauty of the place was lost to Mark today. The familiar area was barely recognizable as Mark drove slowly up the drive. Looking back to view the area from which he had just come, layers of dark smoke hung heavily over the town, obliterating large portions from his view.

The road and the beach were indistinguishable. Even the buildings and trees were merely darker shades of gray or brown. Mark's eyes were beginning to sting and tears blurred his vision. Without air-conditioning, he knew it would have been impossible to have traveled the once familiar road. He looked around and felt he had been picked up and dropped on a distant planet where everything was colorless and drab, a monotonous Martian landscape of ashen hues.

Angus was clearly frightened as he rocked back and forth on his front paws, making low whining noises. Mark spoke to his anxious friend in soft, comforting tones.

With a great sense of relief Mark continued up the monastery drive. Past the gate, halfway up the hill, the drive forked to the right and brought him into the enclosed compound surrounding the chaplain's cottage. Easing his tall frame from the small car, he walked stiffly to a wooden statue of the Madonna and Child. He smiled at the familiar face as it seemed to greet him.

Reaching behind the statue, he found the house key right where he knew it would be. Unlocking the gate to the enclosed courtyard, he walked across worn terracotta tile to the front door. Angus began sniffing and scratching around the foundation of the house.

"Not now, boy. Let's get our gear in before vespers begin. There will be plenty of time for hunting and exploring later."

Before unpacking, Mark phoned the monastery to let the sisters know he had arrived. The childlike voice of Sister Frances answered the phone on the second ring.

"Oh, Father, praise God. We were all so worried that you might not make it through the fire. Please come up and I'll buzz you in. Mother Benedicta will meet you in the first speak-room. I'm so glad you are here safe."

Mark reasoned that he could get settled in later. He stopped only long enough to fill Angus' water and food bowls.

"Take care of the house, old man," he said, patting Angus on the head. "I'll be back in a short while." Hurrying along the cypress-lined drive to the monastery, he looked out over the hills and saw smoke hanging heavy over the Del Monte Forest.

Mark rang the bell and the familiar voice of Sister Frances spoke to him again, this time through the intercom.

"Good afternoon…Father Ross?"

"Yes, Sister Frances, it's me."

"Welcome, Father, please come in. Mother Benedicta is expecting you."

The door buzzed and clicked open. Mark stepped over the threshold and seemed to step back in time. The floor was well-worn and well-scrubbed tile. The furniture was very old and of heavy Spanish design. The air was a confusion of beeswax candles, oil soap and the wonderful aroma of fresh, home-baked bread.

Entering the main hall, he saw the "turn" begin to rotate. Walking closer, he noticed a box of hand-painted greeting cards with a note of welcome from Sister Frances.

"These are beautiful. Did you paint them, Sister?"

"Yes, Father, a small welcoming gift. Mother will be with you in just a few minutes."

Mark picked up the package of cards and watched the "turn" slowly begin to revolve back to its original position. He always thought of the "turn" as a large lazy-susan with a wall dividing it in half. This was the only means the sisters had of reaching out to the world, or for the world to reach into the cloister. One would merely place a basket of food or books on his side of the wall and turn the drum-like cylinder to the other.

"Thank you, Sister, I'll make good use of these while I am here."

Taking his cards, Mark began walking towards the speak-room, a small parlor divided by a floor-to-ceiling grille where one could visit the sisters on occasion. The wooden grille was shuttered as a symbolic barrier between "the world" and the enclosed life of a monastic community. Father Mark stood in front of the grille, and as the shutters slid open, the voice of Mother Benedicta greeted him from the other side.

"Praised be Jesus Christ."

"Now and forever," Mark responded according to ancient custom. Before him stood the imposing figure of Mother Superior. Tall for a woman of her generation, the severe lines of her black habit made her even more impressive.

She seemed genuinely delighted to see the young priest. Smiling as she took her seat, the large wooden rosary attached to the leather belt around her waist clattered against the straight-backed chair.

She smoothed the folds of her habit and adjusted her veil in a very ladylike way that caused Mark to smile as he remembered that Mother Superior had once been a well-known actress before entering religious life. Old habits die hard, he thought with amusement.

He settled his six-foot, four-inch frame onto the cane and wicker chair which seemed to have been designed for someone half his size. The chair creaked and groaned with every move he made.

In a flashback, he was seven years old again and his teacher, Sister Bertha, was admonishing the class to be sure to move to the side of their tiny desks to make room for their guardian angels. He grinned as he imagined himself and his angel down to the last round of a game of musical chairs, jockeying for possession of this little chair.

"Welcome, dear Father. We've been looking forward to sharing this month with you. We were afraid that you might not be able to get to us through the fire. It seems to be shaping up into a major disaster." Her smile was so warm and genuine that Mark again was reminded of what a truly loving person Mother Benedicta was.

"It is pretty bad, Mother. But nothing was going to keep me from getting here, even if Angus and I had to hike in. I've been looking forward to my vacation for months. It's been a tough year and a few weeks of Carmel sunshine and surf is just what the doctor ordered."

"Well, glory be to God, you're here now. Sister Theresa has stocked your pantry with provisions and Sister Paula will send some bread over when it comes out of the oven."

"I smelled it when I came in, Mother. There isn't anything greater than the smell of homemade bread."

"Please let us know if there is anything else you need or want to make your stay more comfortable."

Mark seldom had to buy groceries when he visited the monastery. The people of the village had always been very generous to the sisters and the sisters, in turn, took very good care of their chaplains.

The pleasantness of the moment was shattered by the wailing of a fire-engine siren.

"Sounds like reinforcements are arriving," Mark said. "I saw the smoke as soon as I reached the coast road, but I had no idea it was so close to the monastery. Do you think it might reach here?"

"The coast road is closed just north of Big Sur and firefighters from all over the state are here to help our local people," Mother said. "We were very concerned for the hospital when we heard that the fire had spread to the Del Monte Forest. Some of our sisters went out yesterday and hung several blessed St. Michael medals from the trees along our property."

Mother Benedicta spoke with a quiet air of confidence. "Of course, our sisters could not leave the convent grounds, but a dear friend of our monastery who so often takes care of our needs outside these walls took a few medals with her after Mass yesterday and placed them in the trees along the hospital grounds. It seemed so much simpler to place the hospital in St. Michael's protection than to evacuate the entire building."

Obviously, the fire does not stand a chance against the sisters and St. Michael, Mark thought with a smile.

"Mother, if the safety of the hospital is in the hands of St. Michael and your prayers, I'm sure it will be spared," he said.

"Father Joseph was sorry that he could not wait to see you, Father, but he was quite concerned that he would not be able to get back to San Francisco due to the fire and he had appointments to keep," Mother noted. "We sent him off with a St. Michael, too," she smiled. "Jim and Adele Van Dusen left for Palm Springs just before the fire began last week, but I'm sure their house is safe. Before they left, they asked me to tell you that they had left a guest pass for you at the Country Club."

"That was very kind of them, Mother. I like to use the swimming pool at the Club. The ocean is a bit too chilly for my taste," Mark said. "A walk along the beach is as close as I like to come to these waters."

"I know how much you like walking the beach, Father, but please be very careful. We had a tragic accident last week---one of the teachers at the high school drowned just across the road from us at Monastery Beach, may God rest her soul."

"How tragic, Mother, that such a beautiful place should have such dark history. How many lives, I wonder, have already been lost there?"

"I know, Father," the nun replied. "We pray regularly for the poor souls who met death almost literally on our doorstep."

"It's scary to think of dying out there all alone."

"Maybe they were not as alone as we might suppose, Father. Sometimes it's a comfort to me to think that perhaps the last thing they saw before they left this life was the cross on top of our chapel tower."

"You know, Mother, it still amazes me how people who live behind walls, watch no television and read no newspapers know so much about what's happening in the world around them."

"I used to think the same thing myself forty years ago, before I entered the cloister. I had a rather naïve vision of the monastic life when I was living the Hollywood party circuit in those days. If I gave any thought at all to cloistered life, it was to imagine nuns as serenely out of touch with the real world. I'm sure that most people would be surprised at how much 'reality' slams up against our doors. We are only too often reminded of the real world through the constant flow of requests for prayers that keep flooding in. Letters, postcards, phone calls and visitors keep us informed of what is going on."

The nun continued, "I spent the first decade I was here learning that the true vocation of a cloistered nun is not running away from the world, but to spend one's life in undistracted union with God praying for the world."

The mention of Hollywood reminded Mark of Mother Benedicta's somewhat colorful past. She had been a well-known film star of the fifties. After her fiancee's death in a plane crash, she left the funeral and drove up the coast from Hollywood. She got as far as Carmel and, looking up into the hills, she got her first glimpse of the Moorish-looking towers of the monastery.

She spent several weeks with the sisters, healing and praying, walking in the gardens, and resurrecting her Catholic faith. After a month, she asked for permission to stay, but a wise Mother Superior sent her back to Hollywood. Back to her world of glamour and excitement, with the advice to continue praying and when she was very, very sure, she was to return to the convent for more discernment.

Mother Angela told her that she must face her grief in her normal environment and not hidden away in a convent. She did go back to Hollywood, but after a short time she returned to Carmel. That was forty years ago and she was still here.

In any world, Mother Benedicta's outgoing and cheerful personality would have made her a charismatic leader. In the parlance of religious life, there was an axiom that "grace builds on nature." Forty years of life behind monastery walls had not erased Mother Benedicta's natural vivaciousness, but rather, added an underlying current of serenity that flowed through her words and actions.

Old Hollywood friends visiting the monastery through the years would recognize her characteristic effervescence, but now purified and elevated by the presence of something new and mysterious.

Mark personally knew each of the twenty-one sisters, and he was well aware that they were not all stamped from the same cookie cutter. Each sister had her own unique personality and her own story to tell. These "Brides of Christ" were the most joyful people he had ever known. They had come from all walks of life; many had led very successful professional lives before arriving here. For instance, it was almost unknown that Sister Paula had spent her earlier life in the courtrooms as a criminal lawyer.

As the two friends sat in the gathering gloom of late afternoon, catching up on the events and challenges of the past year, the room seemed illuminated by a source of light other than the fading glow from the chandelier above. Their lively and animated conversation was frequently punctuated by outbursts of laughter. They radiated a genuine joy that people not familiar with the religious life would have thought alien to a life or poverty, chastity and obedience.

The vesper bells began to ring, calling the sisters to evening prayer.

"You must excuse me, Father, I am being paged," Mother Benedicta said with a twinkle in her eye. "The tenth-century version of the pager you know," she said, indicating the tolling bells.

She stood to leave and the wooden grille closed, leaving Mark alone on his side of the room. He left the speak-room and slowly walked through the silent corridor to exit through the chapel. He was about to step into the darkening chapel when he heard the voice of Sister Frances speaking through the "turn."

"Father, we just received word that the fire has been contained. God has heard our prayers."

"That's good news, Sister. Score another one for St. Michael."

Exiting the chapel he was overwhelmed by the beauty of a spectacular California sunset, colors filtered as through a prism by the lingering smoky haze. He stood for a few minutes at the top of the church steps and watched with a sense of joy as the giant orange ball slipped silently into the teal, blue-green waters of the Pacific.

Chapter 3

At dawn the next morning, purifying ocean breezes were sweeping the stench and smoke from the coastal area. The only visible reminder of the fire was the smog that still clung to the hills. Standing in the garden Mark looked to the east and watched an extraordinary sunrise breaking over the mountains above the level of smog. God's in his heaven, all's well with the earth, he thought.

By seven o'clock Mark was in the chapel sacristy, vested and waiting for the bell to stop tolling to begin Mass. Checking himself in the closet mirror, he was glad he had remembered to bring his own alb and some of his vestments with him. His first year he had learned the hard way that it was impossible for a man six-feet, four-inches tall to fit into Father Denis' shorter vestments.

He peeked out the sacristy door into the chapel and saw a dozen familiar faces who came in from the village every morning to join the nuns for Mass. On Sunday the attendance could climb to over two hundred vacationers and villagers.

Over the years, Mark had developed quite a few friendships with these people. They were his summer family. The first face he always looked for was Chloe Martin's. Once his teacher at Berkeley she was now an old friend. She celebrated life with a breathless sense of urgency in a slightly English accent. She was a brilliant teacher, but definitely an acquired taste, handicapped by what her stuffier academic colleagues would characterize as a "regrettable excess of personality."

Entering the chapel, Mark genuflected before the altar. Turning around to face the congregation, he almost burst into laughter when he caught his first glimpse of her. Chloe's ensemble was a collage from Saks Fifth Avenue and the local thrift store. She was wearing a beautiful brocade skirt, accompanied by an outrageous orange peasant blouse. On her feet she wore imitation Birkenstock sandals.

All this was topped off with several strands of faux pearls. Her auburn hair was a shade that could only have come from a bottle. He smiled broadly. Mark had often wondered if Chloe wasn't deliberately caricaturing herself, beating her critics to the punch and doing a better job at it than anyone else could.

They had been fast friends ever since he had taken her "Art and Archaeology" class while working on his undergraduate degree in Anthropology at Berkeley. She was a widow whose husband had died during the Korean War, leaving her childless. She channeled much of her maternal energy toward her students, who may not have always agreed with her philosophy or politics but were, nevertheless, thrilled and entertained by her intensity.

She was a militant in every sense of the word, whose intellect had been honed in the charged and hostile environment of Berkeley's faculty lounges. She was more than a match for the historical revisionists and neo-marxists who pontificated from the academic pulpits provided them at taxpayers' expense.

After Mass, they made arrangements to meet for breakfast in the village at the "Little Swiss Café." Mark loved the Old World charm of the place, but more importantly, he was addicted to their strawberry cheese blintzes. The coffee arrived and Mark filled his nostrils with its steamy aroma.

He looked up from his first satisfying swallow just in time to see Agatha and Paul Gireaux walk in. Part of the "Monastery Breakfast Club," Mark had met them through Chloe years ago. They owned one of the seventy-two art galleries that drew collectors to Carmel from all over the country. In their fifties, they made a handsome couple.

Paul, in his tweed jacket and turtleneck with just the right touch of silver gracing his temples and beard, looked like a model. Agatha was immaculate in a fawn-colored suede suit with her platinum hair swept up in a French twist. They were as sophisticated and urbane as Chloe was Bohemian.

Paul extended his hand toward Mark. "Father Mark, good to see you again. Welcome back to Carmel. A lot of your fans have been looking forward to those sermons of yours."

"Paul, you missed your calling. You should have gone into politics."

Agatha leaned toward Mark, and he kissed her on the cheek in greeting. Her perfume drifted around her as she spoke. He inhaled the familiar scent and was reminded again that it was her own special blend that she had made up for herself alone.

"Father, you have been missed. We enjoy all of Father Denis' replacements. Each one is special, but I confess, we do have our favorites. We enjoy catching up on all your adventures. All of you are like the swallows returning to Capistrano each year for a little sunshine and rest. Sometimes just a glance will tell me what kind of year it has been for you."

"Well, what does the appearance of this weathered sparrow tell you?"

"You got here just in the nick of time," Paul observed with a chuckle. "A few days on the beach will but the fluff back into your feathers. Then you'll be as good as new."

Mark raised his coffee mug in salute. "To Carmel. If only you could bottle this place---its sights and scents, colors and sounds---you could sell it as a tonic to the world-weary. If I were any more relaxed, I'd be comatose."

"And yet we do have our share of high drama, even here in the land of the lotus eaters," said Chloe. Knowing glances passed around the table as the waitress arrived with the blintzes.

When she was safely out of earshot, Chloe continued. "We could have used your services about a week ago, Mark. One of our young teachers was found dead, floating among the rocks near Monastery Beach."

"Yes, Mother Benedicta mentioned something about it yesterday," Mark said.

"Poor Janet. I feel sick every time I think about it. Actually, we knew each other. She was the one who got me to volunteer at the high school teaching an art class. You know how it is when the bean counters whip out their calculators---the arts are the first things to be eliminated. Janet Wayland was the kind of teacher I like to think that I was. She cared about kids and refused to let the bean counters shortchange them."

"But what was she doing swimming at Monastery Beach?" Mark asked. "If she lived here she must have known about the riptides. There are signs posted all over the beach."

"She wasn't swimming. She was found fully clothed. People are talking suicide, but I don't buy that. I'm sure it was an accident," Chloe answered.

"She really was a sweet girl, always so pleasant when she came into the gallery to browse," Agatha added. "I recognized her right away when I saw her picture in the paper. I remember she always seemed drawn to any painting with a dog in it or some other animal. I think she had a love for the little things, the helpless things in life."

Paul interrupted, "That reminds me, Father, do you still have that Scottie of yours?" Mark nodded.

"Well, you'd better keep a close eye on him while you are down here this month. We've had some very bizarre things happen around the village since you were here last. Sick things. I don't even like to mention it because I know how you feel about dogs, but we've had at least a half a dozen ritual animal mutilations in the past few months. Dogs with their ears and tails cut off and eyes gouged out, cats crucified. Mostly down around the Highland south of Point Lobos. But we've had some things happen around here, too. Ironically, we wouldn't have known the extent of it but for the fire which burned away a lot of the underbrush. The firefighters and police have been making grisly discoveries all week."

Suddenly Mark lost his appetite for the blintzes. "That's the sort of thing I'd expect to read about up in my neck of the woods. It has gotten so bad that there is a ban on the adoption of black cats from the animal shelter during the month of October. Did you know that there is now a listing in the yellow pages in San Francisco for the 'Church of Satan'? It is listed under churches along with all the others. It's a sad symptom of where we are when the

Church of Satan has enough credibility to be listed in the telephone book."

Paul reached for the coffee pot to refill Mark's cup. "Father, I have always been amazed at how otherwise intelligent people could be seduced by such nonsense. For example, there is a new bookstore that opened up this year in the village. It's called 'Crystal Visions.' It's filled with occult paraphernalia: crystal balls, tarot cards, new-age books and Ouija Boards. It's over on Serra Street. They seem to do a pretty brisk business, too. And you'd be surprised at how many times I've caught a glimpse of people I recognize from Sunday Mass at the monastery coming and going from that place."

Paul spoke with a tone of indignation. "I always thought that Catholicism was incompatible with such superstition. The Church used to warn us about such things. I can remember my grade school teacher telling us that it was a sin even to have our fortunes told."

Paul punctuated his words by wagging his finger like a spinsterish old-maid schoolteacher. "Come to think of it, you're the only priest I have ever heard talk about the dangers of the occult from the pulpit in my entire adult life. Aren't priests interested in evil anymore?" Paul arched his eyebrows in a questioning way.

"Well, Paul, I think it's that most priests are more concerned with the kind of evil that you can see. For most of them there is enough sin and evil right here in front of us to keep us busy without having to look for it in the realm of the supernatural."

Mark shrugged his shoulders, "Maybe I take it more seriously because of my background in Anthropology. When you encounter such similar legends from culture to culture, when you keep running into almost identical artistic depictions of demons from Ancient Rome to Medieval Europe, from Tibet to Native American petroglyphs in the Southwest, you begin to wonder. I am familiar with all the psycho-babble about demons being products of deranged minds or the manifestation of man's collective unconscious. But what if they're not?"

He paused for a moment to collect his thoughts, and went on. "We know that in the last five years, we have seen an unprecedented rise in the number of requests for exorcisms around the world. Among others, the Archdioceses of Rome and New York have doubled the number of priests working as full-time exorcists in the last five years. The Catholic Church takes this whole subject very seriously. Granted, just because someone thinks he is possessed doesn't necessarily mean that he is. The mental institutions are filled with people who think they are George Washington."

"But how can we tell the difference between possession and just plain mental illness?" asked Paul, slowly lifting his coffee mug.

"Exactly," said Chloe. "I had a cousin who was convinced that he was Sherlock Holmes. He would dress up, complete with deerstalker hat, a calabash pipe and magnifying glass. He became sort of a town mascot, continually prowling around the library, cemetery and police station in search of clues. I've traveled around the world, Mark. I've spent years in the field as a cultural anthropologist, living in huts, talking to shamen, studying primitive peoples. I've been initiated into more than a few tribal secret societies, and I've never yet seen anything that could not be explained physically or psychologically. And I've seen a lot."

"I agree with you, Chloe, but there is still that small percent that you just can't explain away rationally. I do believe that some events are evil personified. I do believe that sometimes a person can be possessed---and so does the Church."

"Tell me, Mark, just how does one go about getting an exorcism?" asked Paul with a smile on his face. Mark felt that his friends were having a little fun at his expense.

"Before the Church will authorize an exorcism, a formal investigation is undertaken involving doctors and psychiatrists as well as priests," Mark explained. "Ninety percent of these investigations end with a diagnosis of mental or physical illness or fraud. But the remaining ten percent are more difficult to explain."

He went on. "For instance, one of the signs of genuine possession that the Church looks for is strange, inexplicable marks, letters or words that appear mysteriously on the victim's body. Also, the ability of the victim to speak in languages of which he or she had no previous knowledge. I remember reading recently about a case of possession that took place in Ireland. It involved a five-year-old child who, among other strange things, started babbling one day in a language that no one could understand. It turned out that the child was speaking an archaic form of Greek that hasn't been heard for about two thousand years."

Despite the warmth of the morning sun pouring in through the leaded windows, the conversation seemed to cast a pall of gloom over the table.

"Did Father Denis tell you that Our Lady of Victory Church in Pacific Grove was broken into and desecrated a few months ago?" Agatha asked the priest.

"No, he didn't mention it."

"Someone got in one night and sawed the crucifix over the main altar in half. They said that an attempt had also been made to break into the tabernacle, but the vandals failed or were frightened off before they could get in. I imagine they were trying to get to the consecrated hosts for some sacrilegious purpose."

"If they were Satanists, they needed the hosts for a Black Mass," said Mark.

"A Black Mass?" queried Agatha.

"A Black Mass is a sacrilegious parody of the Catholic Mass that Satanists perform at their Sabbath to worship Satan. They use a naked woman as an altar and even chant certain Christian prayers backwards, substituting the name of Satan for God or Christ. They need a validly consecrated host, stolen from a Catholic Church to carry out their blasphemous liturgy."

"By the pricking of my thumb, something wicked this way comes. Satan comes to Carmel, film at eleven," Paul said lightheartedly.

"My treat," Chloe said as she picked up the bill. "The Monastery Breakfast Club is hereby adjourned." She laughed, trying to join in with Paul in raising their spirits.

Mark stood on the sidewalk outside of the café, waving good-bye to his friends. As he turned to walk to his own car, he noticed a young woman of seventeen or eighteen watching him from across the street. She was staring at him with such a peculiar intensity that he wondered if she might be one of his parishioners from the monastery. Perhaps she just isn't used to seeing a Roman collar on the streets of Carmel, he thought. When she realized he had seen her, she looked away and quickly disappeared into one of the shops.

After eight years as a priest, Mark was still struck by the power of the collar to attract attention, welcomed and unwelcomed alike. On more than one occasion, his collar had been noticed in a restaurant or airplane terminal and he had been asked on the spot to hear a confession or give some spiritual advice.

The sight of a priest could bring out the best or the worst in people. Mark still experienced a twinge whenever he remembered one sunny summer afternoon, standing in front of his church in full priestly vestments, when a middle-aged man, eyes blazing with hate, walked up to him and spit in his face.

But it was the beauty of the scenery before him that attracted his attention now. It was one of those glorious autumn days that made him fall head over heels in love with Carmel all over again, devil or not.

To Mark it always seemed that his senses were sharper here, more awake. The colors were brighter and sounds clearer. Carmel had a unique perfume all its own. The ocean breeze was redolent with the fragrance of pine and cypress. The sights and scents rushed upon him now, filling him with the sheer joy of being alive.

Here, nature had achieved a perfect balance of shadow and light, of sea and sky, of mountain and forest. The quaint shops and gingerbread houses seemed to have been magically transported from the pages of a child's fairytale book. Little Tudor cottages housed the art galleries and exclusive boutiques for which Carmel was known.

For a town whose Chamber of Commerce had recently boasted that "Nothing sold here is a necessity...we try to offer the finer things in life," Carmel had very humble beginnings.

It got its start as one of the original twenty-one California missions founded by the Franciscan padres in the eighteenth century. It was easy to see why Father Junipero Serra had chosen his mission in Carmel, San Carlos Borromeo, to be his headquarters. He established his chain of missions along the coast one day's march from each other so that he could visit them on foot and more personally supervise this extraordinary enterprise.

A tireless missionary, his life was one of constant travel, but he always returned home to Carmel. And there he remains to this day, interred beneath the sanctuary of his beloved mission.

Mark loved to pray there. Blessed Junipero Serra's serene and benevolent spirit seemed to permeate the whitewashed adobe walls hung with cascades of scarlet and purple bougainvillea. How ironic, thought Mark, that a place founded as an outpost of the Kingdom of God to save souls has become an elite enclave of the wealthy.

Mark smiled as he thought of how Carmel got started. After the great San Francisco earthquake of 1906, the village began to acquire its reputation as an artist's colony when some of the more Bohemian types from the devastated city made their way south to escape their creditors. Some said that was the real reason behind the fact that until very recently, Carmel's cottages had no house numbers on them. The absence of street names and addresses made the bill collector's task that much more difficult. In those days Carmel was a place to disappear and start over again.

Fortunately for Mark, he found his car next to an expired meter just seconds before a meter maid in her scooter, like an avenging Valkyrie, swooped into the lane, gleefully chalking tires. As he headed toward the beach at the foot of Ocean Avenue, he drew in a deep breath and thought, Ah, Carmel. If heaven isn't better than this, I'm not going.

Chapter 4

The young novices waved to Mark from the parapet that ran along the monastery roof. On beautiful days like this, Sister Gerard, the novice mistress, would sometimes take the novices to the roof for an outdoor class on prayer or mystical theology.

It was a clear, brisk day and without their white veils whipping in the wind, they might have been any other group of young women out on a Saturday morning enjoying the warm California sunshine caressing their upturned faces.

Mark shouted up at them, "Be careful, Sisters--- another gust of wind like the last one and you'll all be doing your own rendition of "The Flying Nun." The younger sisters giggled, but Sister Gerard, who had been in the convent for forty years just looked confused.

Mark turned with a final wave and left the sea gazers to continue their metaphysical musings, although he had a feeling that Sister Gerard's explanations of St. John of the Cross and St. Teresa of Avila would have a hard time competing with the pristine beauty of the view spreading out before them.

He entered the walled courtyard that led to the chaplain's cottage and was immediately assailed by the sour smell of decay. He thought he had gotten a whiff of something rotten when he first arrived the day before, but now it was unmistakable. It smelled like something had died.

Mark followed his nose to the crawl space under the house. It was covered by a wooden lattice that served as an access panel. The putrid stench was definitely strongest here. There were signs that Angus had been busy digging here in his absence. Mark entered the cottage and phoned the monastery.

"Good morning, Mother Benedicta. I seem to have a little problem here." He related the situation to the Mother Superior and smiled at her response.

"Not exactly the 'odor of sanctity,' eh Father? I think I know what the problem is. Sister Gemma put some rat poison out last week---Father Joseph had complained about the pitter patter of little feet in the night. Sounds like Sister Gemma's efforts were successful. Will you be out of the house for a couple of hours anytime today?"

"Well, I was thinking about taking a morning run," he answered.

"That would be fine, Father---you go for your run and we'll take care of the problem before you return. Will you leave Angus?"

"No, I think I'll take him along. After the long drive down from the city he needs the exercise as much as I do."

"By the way, Sister Paula has some fresh bread ready for you. She'll leave it on the kitchen counter while you're out."

Saying good-bye, Mark hung up the phone with a smile on his face. Changing into his running shorts and shoes, Mark did some stretching exercises in the driveway and then headed off at a slow clip down Highway One toward Point Lobos two miles south.

Now a State Park, in the last century its sheltered coves had provided safe anchorage for the whaling ships that prowled the California coast. It was a mysterious place of moss-shrouded forest and strange outcroppings of ancient stones that looked as if they might have stood in silent witness since the very dawn of creation itself.

There were ancient Indian legends about this emerald promontory. It was believed to be an abode of demons and earth-bound spirits denied a place in the Happy Hunting Grounds of the hereafter. Tangled thickets of manzanita evoked the twisted shapes of tortured souls forever frozen somewhere between time and eternity. Long before the Spaniards sailed past Point Lobos, it was a place to be avoided.

The late morning sun was high in the sky by now and hot. Mark was sweating by the time he left the highway and turned into the park. Passing the guard booth, he waved to the ranger, a petite young woman trying very hard to look official in her outsized hat and crisp new uniform.

Jogging along well-worn paths into the shadowed stands of Cypress, the sudden coolness sent a shiver down Mark's spine. It wasn't long before the busy sounds of the highway faded away behind him. Even though Mark knew the road was only a few hundred yards away and that there must be dozens of tourists all through the park, he was suddenly overcome by a sense of complete isolation.

Just a few minutes off the beaten path, surrounded by chest-high walls of tangled brush and waving curtains of Spanish moss, he felt utterly alone.

Normally he would have felt grateful for the peace and privacy, relieved from the constant crush of human beings and human needs that constantly pressed up against him like a musty fug on a sticky day.

Instead, the absence of man-made noise made him feel strangely anxious. He never thought of himself as one of those people who spooked easily. In fact, his take-charge nature and ability to remain calm in the face of crisis had earned him the nickname "Warden" by his friends in college.

So this odd and creeping sense of vulnerability suddenly seemed utterly irrational. Nevertheless, he had to admit to himself that he would have felt greatly consoled by the sound of human laughter or a radio playing softly somewhere off in the distance. Just some comforting human racket to let him know he was not alone.

Isn't it around here that Paul said some of those poor tortured animals were found? Mark wondered.

He forced the hideous images of crucified cats and dismembered dogs from his mind. He decided enough was enough and shifted his run into high gear, taking a turn that he knew would take him back to the park's main road. As he ran he couldn't shake the feeling that he was being watched.

The place itself seemed charged with an unseen presence---conscious, alive. The echo of pounding waves reverberating around him created the impression of breathing, giant lungs---inhaling and exhaling.

Daylight filtered through the branches, creating a filigree pattern. Like a feather floating over the face of some snoring giant, wafting up and then floating down, the Spanish moss waved in the trees, keeping time with the crashing waves.

Paul's story had intensified the eerie feeling of the place. Coupled with half-remembered legends, it was all beginning to play havoc with Mark's imagination, and he knew it. His mood was even beginning to rub off on

Angus, who started rumbling in a long, low growl as he ran at the priest's side.

"Come on, Fuzz Face, I think we've both had enough for now," Mark said, turning back to the monastery. Emerging from the cool, green darkness was like shaking off slimy, subterranean tentacles. The blanket of sunshine warming the chill from his back never felt so good. It was like climbing out of a grave.

By the time he returned to the monastery, he was drenched with perspiration. The sight that greeted him as he stepped through the gate into the courtyard reminded him of Dorothy's first glimpse of the Ruby Slippers in the "Wizard of Oz"---two sneaker shod feet protruded from the crawl space beneath his house. A loud whirring noise from a portable wet-vac was occasionally broken by a thunking noise as it swallowed up the little mouse corpses.

"Whirr...thunk...whirr...thunk", Mark cringed as he listened to the appliance-turned-undertaker.

The noise came to a halt and Mark offered a prayer of thanksgiving. Sister Gemma backed out from under the house, her San Francisco Giants baseball cap set askew atop her veil. Sneakers replaced the sandals that were part of her normal habit.

Sister Gemma, all four feet, eight inches of her, standing at attention like a soldier with the wet-vac's extension tube over her shoulder, presented Mark with a picture that only endeared her more to him.

She had been here longer than any of the other sisters, having arrived on her seventeenth birthday, sixty-five years ago. Perhaps it was her advanced years that caused Mother Benedicta to give in to her little idiosyncrasies, such as the sneakers and baseball cap, which he knew for a fact she never wore to chapel.

When the wet-vac had been donated to the sisters, Sister Gemma made it her own personal apostolate. She had found more uses for the monster than its makers had ever dreamed of.

"There you are, Father." She smiled up at him. "I think that should take care of the smell."

"Thank you, Sister Gemma, and please thank Mother for me."

"I will, Father."

"Have a nice day," he said.

She gathered up her equipment and Mark watched as the diminutive nun walked back toward the whitewashed monastery and disappeared into the cloister through a garden door cut into the wall. Peter Pan, he thought, that's who she reminds me of, Peter Pan. She really is straight out of central casting.

A hot shower was definitely the next order of business after his run. He glanced at the clock as he passed through his bedroom. It was nearly noon and he wanted to get in a little swim before lunch at the Club. It's a tough life, he thought with a smile, but someone's got to do it.

Stepping out of the shower, Mark wrapped a towel around his midriff and stepped on the scale. Through a steady regimen of exercise and running he had managed to hold his weight at two hundred, the same weight he had carried when he entered the seminary.

He ran his hand through a still wet shock of black hair. His dark features were a striking contrast to his pale blue eyes. When the older Irish ladies of his parish gathered for tea, they gossiped among themselves that their pastor must be of the "Black Irish" descended from the shipwrecked Spanish sailors of the Armada who washed up on Ireland's shores.

Mark hurriedly dressed in a pair of faded, slim-cut jeans, top-siders and salmon-colored shirt with the sleeves rolled up---the kind of outfit that would have caused some of his little old Irish ladies to raise an eyebrow or two. The telephone rang.

"Hello."

"What's new, venerable Father?" Chloe teased. "Had enough solitude for awhile? Do you have any plans for today?"

"Nothing that can't be changed. I just finished my run and was about to go out and get some firewood for tonight. You know I have my little rituals when I'm down here. If I had a fireplace back at the rectory I'd probably build a fire every night---rain or shine."

"Well, how about taking a break? What do you say we meet in the village for coffee?"

"Fine, but let's make it lunch, I'm starved."

"How about the Old Forge in about thirty minutes?"

"Fine. I'll see you there."

Guess there's no swimming today, Mark thought.

Finding a parking space in Carmel was almost as difficult as finding one in San Francisco. The steady stream of tour buses and visitors created daily traffic jams that were no small annoyance for the villagers. At night it was a different story.

The fog-shrouded streets of the tiny village often seemed deserted. Here and there some cars could be found parked in front of the quaint but pricey restaurants. But when the shops closed around six, the streets were, by and large, empty.

Mark decided to walk into town, taking a shortcut along the beach, past the old mission, and through a cypress-shaded neighborhood. Most of the old clapboard-covered cottages were one-story and almost all of them were surrounded by gray picket fences tinkered together from old pieces of weathered driftwood.

There were no sidewalks along the winding lanes, only a blanket of soft, moist earth and pine needles. The twisting path eventually brought him to Junipero Serra street and Carmel's commercial district in the heart of the village.

On the other side of Ocean avenue, next to a small park, was the Old Forge restaurant. From the patio, Chloe watched Mark as he sprinted across the busy street. As she waved him over to her table, the sleeves of her orange and black caftan billowed in the breeze. She sprang from her chair, nearly knocking it over, and greeted him with a quick peck on both cheeks.

"Hey, people will talk," Mark jested, his face reddening.

"Let 'em."

Mark picked up a napkin from the table and wiped the crimson smudges from his cheeks.

"What do you think of my outfit, dear boy?"

"Colorful."

"Orange and black, I try to stay in step with the season. You don't think it's over the top, do you?"

"Chloe, if you were wearing bib-overalls we'd be drab little sparrows compared to you."

"Thank you, dear boy. Now that we've settled the question of whether it's the clothes that make the man or the man...or woman...that makes the clothes, let me ask, how are you?"

"Just dandy, but you know how it is, it takes awhile to settle into a new routine. I never sleep well the first couple of nights away from home."

"Tell me about it, dear one. I can't believe that I used to spend months on end sleeping on a cot under a mosquito net in Africa, Haiti or some such place. I've become so attached to my own bed that if I go to San Francisco for the symphony or opera, I'd rather drive all the way home rather than sleep in a motel."

"Are you still raising pigeons? Don't they keep you awake with their constant racket?"

"Doves, if you please, not pigeons. And no, they don't disturb me in the least. In fact, I find their soft cooing to be very soothing."

"Well, one small black dog is about as much as I can cope with. Besides, when it comes to pets, I prefer something that can love me back."

"And what makes you think my doves don't love me? Their much more sensitive than people might think. I believe animals have a rich emotional life, more than we humans give them credit for. I'm convinced they feel things that we are impervious to. My doves always let me know when an earthquake is about to happen. They become agitated and they won't eat."

"Did the fire affect them?"

"The smell of the smoke nearly drove them crazy. They flapped around their coops so violently I thought they were going to injure themselves. They haven't calmed down yet."

"Knowing how you love your pigeons, excuse me, your doves, you must have been distressed about the mutilated animals the fire turned up. Paul said the firemen suggested they might have been sacrificed."

"Well, I wouldn't go so far as to use the word 'sacrifice'. That would imply an interpretation, a value judgment brought to the event by the observer---something a scientist, like an anthropologist, should never do. Didn't I teach you anything in Anthropology 101 at Berkeley? All you can say is that the firefighters discovered some animals that appear to have been slaughtered."

"Come on, Chloe, with all your experience in primitive religions, I think you'd be a little bolder in offering an 'interpretation'."

"I hope by 'primitive' you mean earliest and not uncivilized, dear boy."

"You taught at Tulane in New Orleans, the Voodoo capital of America, for heaven's sake. Chloe, you are an expert on West African religions and how they blended with Catholicism to become Voodoo and Santeria in the New World. It just seems to me that that entitles you to venture a judgment or at least an interpretation. Haven't you seen this sort of thing before?"

"Well, in the first place, I haven't personally seen whatever it is the firefighters were supposed to have found. Besides, my expertise is in West African religions. What they found in the forest sounds more like Satanism. Voodoo may sacrifice animals, it doesn't torture them."

"Here comes our lunch," Mark said. "What say we declare a truce and eat?"

****

After Mass the next morning, Mark changed clothes and grabbed his wallet and keys from the table. He decided his exercise regimen needed a change. Driving through the Carmel gate into the Seventeen Mile Drive, Mark entered a world of wealth and privilege where the residents had managed to turn one of the most stunning sections of California coast into their own private preserve.

The entire road was sealed off with manned guard booths through which only the residents could pass without a fee. Mark flashed his guest pass, courtesy of the Van Dusens, to the watchman and was waved through the gate.

Passing the castles of America's robber barons, Mark felt a sigh of sadness well up in him for the emptiness and the failed dream of happiness that played itself out on the stages of these vast stone villas.

He had been invited into enough of these houses over the years to know the script---the husbands away on too many business trips, the nightly cocktail hour that started at sunset and stretched into unconsciousness, and the forty-something wives on the cusp of crumbled beauty who dulled the panic with combinations of valium and scotch.

They looked for someone to hold their hand and purr that they were still beautiful and safe and appreciated. And there was always someone close at hand to provide whatever was needed, from the gigolo tennis pros in their blinding white togs and equally blinding smiles, to the court jesters who could make the dullest of them feel witty and sparkling.

The emerald slopes of the Del Monte forest began to yield to a different view as Mark began his descent toward the Pebble Beach Country Club.   .

Continuing on through the tangle of Pine and Cypress, patches of Pacific blue were visible. The Beach and Tennis Club was planted squarely in the midst of the buff-colored sand traps and rolling green felt expanses of the golf course. The lawn was so meticulously manicured that it reminded Mark of a huge pool table. As he maneuvered into the Cypress-shaded parking lot, he was aware that he was an interloper on this playground of the rich and famous.

Dressed casually in a pair of walking shorts and a polo shirt, Mark looked like any other member of the exclusive Country Club. After signing in, he headed for the locker room to change into his swim trunks.

The locker rooms were empty, so Mark assumed everyone was in the dining room or on the green. He had the pool all to himself. With an easy athletic grace, he dove into the cool water and swam underneath the surface the entire length of the pool. Mark swam hard and fast back and forth in the lap lane as if he were in an Olympic competition.

Muscles straining, pulse pounding in his head, he kept up his punishing pace until he was exhausted. When his arms finally quit on him, he rolled over onto his back to float and stare up at the clouds. He could feel the tension of the past year begin to slip away in the adrenalin-induced euphoria.

This is just what I need, he thought. A month down here and I should be ready to face the trenches when I go back. He luxuriated in the aquamarine water. It had been a very difficult and busy year; not only was he the pastor of a very busy parish in the inner city, but he also served the police department as chaplain.

Floating weightlessly, enjoying the sensations of warm sun on his face and chill water on his back, the contrast suddenly seemed to him a nice metaphor for his life---two extremes, hot and cold. Ministry in the big city was a life of chaotic intensity that came in staccato, machine gun bursts of activity, punctuated by moments of quiet emptiness.

Returning to the locker room, Mark quickly showered and dressed, eager to see what was on the menu in the dining room. The Pebble Beach Country Club had always enjoyed the services of the finest chefs, and Mark had never been disappointed in the fare. The food was always presented in a manner that was appealing to the eye as well as delicious.

As he entered the dining room, the maitre d' greeted him with a smile that was both friendly and aloof.

"Good afternoon, Father Ross. It is very good to see you again. Will you be dining alone today?"

"Thank you, Emil, it is good to be back. And, yes, I am dining alone today."

"Would you prefer the dining room or the patio?"

"Definitely outside. I don't want to miss a minute of this beautiful weather. We haven't seen much sun up in the City lately."

Emil seated Mark along the railing where he could watch the ocean and the sea gulls as they soared over the whitecaps in their constant search for food. From his vantage point, he could watch the golf enthusiasts chasing their little white balls across the magnificent green expanse

The maitre d' presented the wine list before showing Mark the menu.

"Thanks, Emil, but I think I will order lunch and let you choose the appropriate wine---just a glass. You're the expert when it comes to these matters."

"Very good, Father. May I suggest the fresh salmon. It is particularly fine today."

"Sounds great---and how about a salad with that wonderful house dressing?"

"Yes, sir. Your waitress will be with you momentarily."

Mark leaned back in his chair and took in a deep breath of fresh salt air. He noticed that the gulls had lost their place to a group of pelicans who were dive-bombing head first into the waves in an amazing display of piscatorial skill.

Mark's attention was drawn back to the table as he turned to see a very attractive young girl placing a basket of rolls and a colorful salad before him. As she turned to a service table for a water pitcher to replenish his glass, he thought there was something familiar about her.

Mark made the sign of the cross to begin grace when he noticed the girl staring at him.

"I don't mean to be rude," she said, "but aren't you the priest from the monastery? I saw you a couple of days ago with Mrs. Martin." He remembered now that she was the young girl across the street from the restaurant.

"Yes," Mark said, "I am the visiting chaplain for the month." He sensed that the girl wanted to say something, but she just stood there.

"Father," she began, "I wonder, could I come to see you?" she stammered. "I am a Catholic, but we don't go to church much anymore. Not since my grandmother died. Does that make a difference?"

"No, of course not. You don't have to be a Catholic for us to talk." He smiled at the nervous girl. "But I wouldn't want to upset your parents---would they mind, do you think?"

"No Father, I'm sure they wouldn't care. They are good friends with Father Denis," she explained. "My name is Shelby Townsend and I get off work about three. May I come to see you then?"

"That would be fine, Shelby. Let's say about three-thirty at the chapel."

She left him to his salad, but a gloom seemed to have settled over the afternoon. Somehow his salad wasn't as colorful and the sunshine not as warm. He wondered what could be troubling such a youngster.

From all appearances, she had a lot more going for her than the average teenager that he was accustomed to working with. Most likely she came from a well-to-do family. Most of these part-time jobs at the Club usually went to the children of the members. And she was definitely one of the prettiest girls he had seen in a long while. Lord, I hope she's not another teenage pregnancy, he thought.

When his salmon was served, his spirits perked up a bit. He couldn't help but marvel at the beauty on his plate, a rainbow of color: coral salmon, yellow lemon wedge, small deep purple cabbage leaf garnish with orange carrot curls and the inevitable yellow and green zucchini squash.

Looking at this culinary delight, he thought of Mrs. Murphy back at the rectory. She was a great housekeeper and cook, but her corned beef and cabbage never looked like this.

"It's almost too pretty to eat." His feeble attempt at humor was completely lost on the troubled waitress who seemed totally preoccupied.

She gave him a nervous smile. "Would you care for anything else, Father?"

"No thanks, this is fine. I'll see you about three-thirty."

She smiled shyly and walked away. Mark watched her as she approached another table. He couldn't help but notice the sadness that overshadowed her beautiful, young face. She seemed old beyond her years.

Chapter 5

Mark went straight to the chapel. He sensed that this girl was in real trouble and he would need wisdom greater than his own to help her. He had learned early on in his priesthood that the best way to prepare for a sermon or for a difficult counseling appointment was on his knees before the Blessed Sacrament. It was also a powerful reminder to him that he was a priest, not a social welfare worker.

In the course of his experience as a counselor, he had come to believe that the vast majority of problems people suffered from were self-generated and self-perpetuated by a stubborn unwillingness to change.

It was a grim adherence to self-destructive patterns of thought, behavior and association that reaped a continual harvest of shame and unhappiness.

In the language of Christian tradition, there was a word for this life-saving change of direction--- "repentance."

Yet so few people seemed interested in learning that they held the key to liberation in their own hands, which is why he prayed before his counseling appointments. It was one thing to show a person the way out of hell, but only grace could give a person the courage to make the journey.

The rhythmic pounding of the waves suddenly amplified as the chapel door swung open. Soft footsteps echoing against the clay tile floor approached from behind and then halted. A scarcely audible voice behind his right ear whispered, "Father?"

He turned around and was surprised to find himself looking into the young and beautiful face of Shelby

Townsend. He looked at his watch, only then realizing that nearly three hours had passed since he had left her at the Club. He motioned for her to sit in the pew next to him. In a face that could have easily graced the cover of any fashion magazine, her eyes were her most attractive feature. Warm and soft, they seemed to be lit by a kindness that one wouldn't normally have expected to see in one so young.

Those eyes now darted nervously around the empty church, and only when she was satisfied that they were alone did she take her seat next to him. Sensing her anxiety, Mark prayed silently that God would show him the way to help this frightened young woman.

Hesitantly, she started to speak. "After Miss Wayland died,…she was my teacher. Well, after she died I was so afraid. I didn't know where to turn or who to go to. Then I saw you outside the restaurant. And when I saw you again in the dining room at the Club, I figured maybe it was a sign. Maybe God was sending me someone who could help me. All I know is that I can't go on being so afraid all the time."

Tears started to well up in those beautiful eyes and she began to tremble.

The priest put his hand reassuringly on her shoulder.

"Go on," he said. "Start from the beginning."

She brushed the hair back from her face and took a deep breath. "It all started last March. There's a house in the Highlands, just a couple of miles from here. No one's lived there for a long time. It's become a place for kids to hang out. It's not easy to see from the road and we've never gotten caught."

She continued, "Sometimes a bunch of us would go there after a game and have a couple of beers together. There's a huge stone fireplace that still works and sometimes it's nice to just sit by the fire and talk with your friends. My boyfriend, Jeff Archer, and I have never gone there alone. I think it would be too scary without the others."

"Well, one Saturday night," she explained, "about a dozen of us ended up there after the game. We beat Salinas and everyone was in the mood to celebrate. One of the girls, Stacy Ballard, brought a Ouija Board. She got it at the new, weird bookstore in the village. Stacy said she had met some interesting people there who were turning her on to some really radical stuff. She kept talking about how amazing it all was and how the Ouija Board was only part of it."

Shelby went on. "It sounded like fun, so we all took turns playing with it. At first, nothing happened and some of the boys started saying 'rip-off' and 'bogus.' But then it started to move. It was kind of scary, but it was fun, too. The board spelled out 'Greetings,' then it said, 'We are with you.' Everyone laughed and said Stacy was pushing the planchette across the board. But when it was my turn, I knew that wasn't so. Father, it really did seem to be moving under it's own power. My fingers were barely resting on it."

The girl became quiet and seemed afraid to continue.

"Go on, Shelby. What happened then?" Mark prompted.

"It began to spell out messages and answer questions. Jeff asked about the following week's game. It predicted we would win and by how many points---And it was right, Father!"

Her voice escalated. "The score turned out exactly as the Ouija Board said it would. It also began to talk about Annie Miller, one of the girls from our class. It said that she was pregnant. Stacy asked it who the father was and all it answered was 'S'." One of the boys with us that night was Scott Dalton, a friend of Jeff's. He is on the basketball team with Jeff. I remember looking at Scott that night and thinking he looked as white as a sheet. Things started getting pretty stupid then. The board just stopped making any sense, spelling out partial words and finally the planchette went to the word good-bye and slid off the edge of the board."

Throughout her narrative the priest remained silent, not wanting to interrupt, a discipline he had learned in the confessional.

"You know, Shelby, a good guess at who's going to win a basketball game by a correct point spread is hardly evidence that you've tapped into the psychic hotline. The bookies do it all the time in Vegas. And you might have been right with your first guess---one of the boys could have been pushing the planchette."

"But Father, there was more to it than that," Shelby interrupted. The very next week Annie Miller had a miscarriage in Ms. Sitkowski's third period P.E. class. Later that day Jeff and I ran into Scott at the A&W. He was totally wasted and told us the baby was his."

Shelby added, "After that, Stacy never stopped talking about the amazing new things she was learning. She told us the power of the Ouija Board was a toy compared to what she was doing now. She would brag that she could have anything and do anything she wanted to now. She began to scare me the way she talked."

She caught her breath. "If anyone was having boyfriend problems or trouble with someone at school, she'd say, 'I could take care of that for you if you'd let me. We could really mess this person up if you wanted to.' Or, if we saw something we liked at the Mall, she'd say, 'I know a way to get anything you want. Anything at all.' She was really acting weird. She seemed different, more serious, not like the old Stacy we'd known. I know it sounds really stupid now, but it was scary and yet at the same time, it was kind of exciting."

She groaned, "Oh, God, why did we do it?" The dam finally broke and Shelby's self-control dissolved into a torrent of tears. Her body shook with deep sobs that echoed through the empty chapel.

Mark felt a deep sense of sympathy for the troubled girl. He gently whispered, "It's all right, Shelby. Everything is going to be all right."

"No, Father, it's not all right," she said with sudden steel in her voice. She wiped the back of her hand across her eyes like a small child. "I don't know if it will ever be all right again! We did it."

"What did you do, Shelby?" Mark felt a shiver run up his spine.

"We let her talk us into trying it."

"Trying what? What did you do?"

"We were thirteen, you see. Just the right number for a coven, she said. We could get anything we wanted if we did what she told us to do. At first it seemed like a game, something different. So we agreed to meet at the old house up in the Highlands. Stacy was already there when we arrived. She had painted this huge circle on the floor around a five-pointed star, with candles burning at each point. They call it a..." she hesitated.

"I know what they call it, Shelby. A pentagram, or sometimes it's called a pentacle."

"That's right, Father, a pentagram. Well, inside the pentagram was a beautiful white dove. It was all tied up with cord and there was a dagger lying next to the poor bird. She told us to take our places inside the circle. I remember thinking it was strange that there were only twelve of us because she had said we needed thirteen to be a coven. Stacy started to read out loud from a book. In a strange way it almost sounded like Church. She kept on invoking the power of the 'Master' and chanting 'as above, so below, as above, so below.' While she was doing this, someone else arrived. Suddenly there was someone standing behind me. Whoever it was had on a long robe and his head was covered with a large hood, so I couldn't see his face."

Shelby explained, "Stacy had each of us say out loud the thing we wanted most. Jeff asked for a red Mustang like his Uncle Larry's. I asked that my parents would get back together. All the other kids had a wish, too. Then, before we knew what was happening, Stacy took the knife and cut the dove's head off. It was awful---the worst thing I ever saw. I left that night feeling so ashamed of what we had done. I swore I would never let anyone ever again talk me into something like that. I told Jeff I would never go back there."

"Shelby, you made a mistake. If there is anything our faith teaches us, it's that God loves us and forgives us. He forgives everything, if we're sorry."

"I believe that, Father, but it's not so simple. Sometimes I am afraid that we made an offer of some kind, an invitation that was accepted. About a week after that night, Jeff's Uncle Larry died unexpectedly and left Jeff his vintage '66 Mustang. It's a classic. But that's not all. My parents split up a year ago, a trial separation they called it. For a long time they were so busy with their careers that I wasn't seeing much of them. And when I did, Mom and Dad always seemed to end up fighting. I was so afraid that we wouldn't be a family anymore. Then, two months ago, Mom and Dad got back together again, just like that. And they are so much happier now. They're even going to counseling. But it's not just Jeff and Scott and me, Father."

Shelby couldn't stop, "Corrine got what she wanted, too, in a twisted sort of way. She was there that night with us. She's always wished that she lived in a bigger, more luxurious house because some of her neighbors had better homes than her family had. When the fire came through her area, her house was the only one spared. So in a way she ended up with the biggest house. All the larger ones burned down. Don't you see what I'm trying to tell you? We all got what we wished for in one way or another."

"Shelby, I am really happy that your folks decided to give it another try. A lot of families have problems these days. It's not unusual for a couple to take some time off from their marriage to sort things out."

"But can't you see, Father? It's because of what happened that night in the old house. We made it happen. I asked for my parents to get together and they did. Jeff got his car. It seems that everyone got the wish that he made that night. I am afraid of what the 'Master' will want in return. I couldn't bear to see my parents split up again."

"Don't you think you might give some credit to your parents and their love for each other, and for you?"

"But what about Jeff?" Shelby persisted.

"So you're saying what? That Satan somehow caused Jeff's uncle to die so that he could inherit his car?

"It isn't just the car, Father. Jeff's changed. It's like he has this superior attitude toward everyone. All of a sudden, according to him, the world is divided into two camps---winners and losers, with the losers definitely being the majority. He wears this strange medallion around his neck, and when I asked him where he got it, he just smiled. There was something in the way he smiled that scared me. It wasn't like Jeff. Some of the others who were there that night have started wearing crystals. Stacy has totally wigged out. She only wears black now and has this way of staring at you that makes you feel all clammy inside."

She sighed, "Jeff gets angry with me because I won't go back to the Highlands with him anymore. I'm sure he is still going there anyway. We used to go out every Saturday night and talk on the phone every day. Now I don't hear from him for days at a time."

"So you think that Jeff and the others are delving into the occult?" Mark asked.

"I know they are, Father."

"How? Because of the medallion?" Mark questioned.

"Because of what I saw happen with my own eyes. It was the Fourth of July. A bunch of us went out to the sand dunes to watch the fireworks from Monterey. One of the guys with us was Pete Hardy. Pete is a real show off, always trying to impress everyone with how great he is. He's a 'been there, done that' kind of person. He has to prove he's faster or stronger or smarter than anyone. That night he was trying to do it with card tricks. When he got over to us, Jeff just smiled and said, 'Answer my riddle and I'll answer yours. Tell me how I do this and I'll tell you how you do your tricks.' Then he held out his hands, palms up. As we watched, faint pink marks began to form on each of his hands. In a few seconds, they started to darken and take on the appearance of deep red welts. A perfect pentagram had formed on each of Jeff's palms. As God is my witness, Father, I am telling you the truth. I know what I saw was real."

Shelby's eyes filled with tears again.

"After that, I was determined to get the truth out of him," she went on.

"He must have been feeling pretty confident after that night in the dunes, because he told me that he and the others had found someone, a teacher, who was showing them how to open doors to a world I couldn't even begin to imagine. I told him that I was scared. That what he was getting into was dangerous and wrong. He went wild. He said that I could either come along with them or else I could join the losers and get out of his way."

She continued, "We had a terrible fight. I said I was afraid for him and I threatened to go tell his parents. He stopped yelling and just stared at me. He was perfectly calm. I've never seen a look like that on anyone's face in my life. All he said was, 'I wouldn't do that if I were you, Shelby. I really wouldn't.' It was like he wasn't Jeff anymore, he was someone I didn't know. I couldn't believe he could change so quickly."

She added, "After that, I started to get the feeling that I was being watched. For months now, I'll look out my bedroom window and there'll be a car parked in the alley below. Sometimes I'm sure it's Jeff's red Mustang, but sometimes it's not. I've heard footsteps behind me in the parking lot at school and sometimes at work, but when I turn around, there's no one there."

Mark commented, "It sounds like someone is trying to frighten you."

"Well, it's working."

"What do your parents think about all this?"

"I haven't told them any of this, Father. I can't," Shelby said. "I'm afraid of what might happen to them if I drag them into this. Especially after what happened to Miss Wayland."

"Wasn't she the teacher who drowned at Monastery Beach last week?" Mark's curiosity was heightened.

"Yes, Father. She was my guidance counselor at school."

"Shelby, what does Miss Wayland have to do with any of this?"

"It was after I found the dead dove."

"Dead dove? Are you talking about the dove they killed at the house that night?"

"No, Father, this was a different bird. I went out to my car one morning and found a brown paper bag on the hood. I opened it and inside was a decapitated dove, completely drained of blood. There wasn't a single drop of blood in that bag, either. That was when I went to Miss Wayland. I had to talk to someone. She was more like a friend than a teacher and I was so frightened. I never meant to hurt her, Father. I really didn't think I was putting her in such danger. Honest."

The monastery bells began tolling for evening prayer. The sisters had invited Mark to lead them in vespers this evening and he suddenly realized that he had only ten minutes to prepare. His attention returned to the frightened you woman next to him.

"So do you think there's a connection between your teacher's death and your friends?"

"Ex-friends, Father, ex-friends. All I know is that Miss Wayland died the very night I told her my story."

She buried her face in her hands and leaned forward until her head almost touched her knees. Her sobbing resounded through the chapel as the priest tried to comfort her.

"It's my fault. It's all my fault," she cried.

"This is a lot to take in, Shelby. We'll need to talk more about this. But I do know that Janet Wayland's death is not your fault. You're not responsible for what happened to her. If all this really happened as you say it did, we'll have to get help. There is a friend of mine that I can talk to about this. He'll know what to do. Would you like me to go with you to see your parents?"

"No, Father, please don't tell them yet."

"All right, it can wait. But will you be all right for now?"

She straightened up and nodded, brushing the tears from her cheeks.

"Remember, Shelby you are not alone. I'll help you. I promise."

Mark reached into his wallet and took out a laminated holy card that he always carried with him. He handed it to her. It was a picture of an angel dressed in the armor of a warrior. In his hands was a spear poised to strike at a hideous, black, bat-winged creature writhing beneath his feet.

Shelby turned the card over and read the prayer printed on the back:

"St. Michael the Archangel, defend us in battle. Be our protection against the wickedness and snares of the devil. May God rebuke him we humbly pray. And do thou, O Prince of the heavenly host, by the power of God, cast into hell Satan and all the evil spirits who roam through the world seeking the ruin of souls."

The priest explained, "St. Michael the Archangel. He's the archenemy of Satan and guardian of God's Church. It was St. Michael who cast Satan from heaven in the great war between the angels. He vanquished Satan once, and he can do it again. Trust in God, Shelby, and mighty forces will come to your aid."

"I will, Father. But please be careful. After what happened to Miss Wayland, I don't want anything to happen to you, too."

The bells continued tolling as the first streaks of crimson graced the sunset sky. Soon it would be twilight.

Chapter 6

"May the grace of our Lord Jesus Christ, the love of God our Father and the fellowship of the Holy Spirit be with you all."

Two hundred and fifty voices thundered back as one. "And also with you."

"Let us call to mind our sins, remembering that God is full of gentleness and compassion," Mark went on. From behind the grille within the sanctuary, hidden from the eyes of all but the priest, the nuns took up the ancient chant of repentance.

"Kyrie eleison. Christe eleison. Kyrie eleison. Lord have mercy. Christ have mercy. Lord have mercy."

Standing outside the front doors of the chapel after Mass, Mark was shaking hands and talking to parishioners as they left. Many old familiar faces and some strange new ones clustered about, welcoming him back or wanting to introduce themselves.

Just when he thought the last of the crowd had departed, he heard a voice from behind. "We seem to attract more than our fair share of holy men to Carmel."

Mark turned. In front of him stood a woman in her early thirties. Sleek and tall, her raven hair pulled back in a sophisticated chignon, she was beautiful in an exotic way that suggested something foreign.

"Marissa Bentley," she said, extending her hand.

"Father Mark Ross. We haven't met before, have we?"

"No, I'm a newcomer to Carmel. I moved here from Scottsdale last year."

"Business or pleasure?" Mark asked.

"Both. I've opened a little bookstore in the village, but I also enjoy the ambiance of the place. I like being around successful people."

"I would think that running a bookstore in a place like Carmel would be a pretty competitive business. We must have at least a half-dozen already that I can think of."

"Well, I guess you could say we cater to a particular clientele. Actually the place is doing quite well. Perhaps you'd like to come by for a visit someday. We have the largest collection of books on spirituality on the peninsula. Really, Father Ross, it's right up your alley."

"Sounds interesting, though I confess that during my vacation I usually confine myself to detective stories, mysteries and spy novels. It's when I get to catch up on all my fun reading."

As they talked, he noticed that she continually fondled a large gold medallion hanging around her neck. Suspended from a long, gold chain, it reached almost to her waist. Black nail polish? Mark thought to himself as he watched those long, tapered fingers caress and curl around the unusual piece of jewelry.

"I found your sermon to be very interesting, even provocative. I can't say I liked everything you had to say, but I found myself strangely moved by the way you said it. I have always found passion to be compelling, even when I think it is wrong."

Mark arched his eyebrows and smiled, "I thank you for that left-handed compliment---I think. But you know I only preach the teaching of the Church. Nothing new or revolutionary here, unless you consider the gospel revolutionary."

"Times change, Father, and the Church must change with them or it will become irrelevant."

"But the truth doesn't change, does it?"

"Truth is a matter of personal perception and experiences, don't you think?" Her voice was taunting. "After all, what's true for you might not be true for me."

"You will forgive me, Miss Bentley, if I say that is a strange attitude for a Catholic to have. The Catholic Church teaches that there is such a thing as objective truth that can be discovered and lived and communicated to others. Ours is a revealed religion, not something each person makes up for himself as he goes along. Jesus Christ is the same yesterday, today and forever."

"And you will forgive me, Father, if I say there are limits to the credibility of a celibate, all-male heirarchy. After all, what do they really have to say to women today? Or to those who aren't afraid to celebrate their sexuality or reach out to claim their own power?" The acid edge in her voice had begun to strip away any semblance of civility.

Seeming suddenly to realize that she had stepped over the line, Marissa Bentley assumed her most charming persona.

"Oh dear, here I go off on my soapbox again. And all I wanted to do was to welcome you. What can I say, Father? Your passion is contagious." She flashed an angelic smile at the priest.

Her hand finally ceased its preoccupation with the medallion and reached into her purse, allowing him his first clear view of it. It was a triangle with a cross at each point, surrounded by a circle. It seemed somehow familiar but he couldn't quite place where he had seen the design before.

From her purse, she produced an embossed business card bearing the same emblem. Handing it to the priest she said, "I would love to continue our discussion. Can I persuade you to visit my humble little establishment?"

"I'll be here all month, and it is a very small town, Miss Bentley. I'm sure our paths will cross again," Mark responded.

There was something almost feline in her manner as she descended the steps toward the parking lot. Mark watched her as she slid into the front seat of a sleek, black Jaguar convertible. Book stores must be a profitable venture, he mused. Powering the engine in a mighty roar, she waved as she turned down the drive toward the highway.

Mark was used to playing verbal volleyball with pick-and-choose Catholics. Twenty years of watered down preaching and teaching had produced an entire generation of religious illiterates who held some bizarre notions about Catholicism. But there was something else in his encounter with Marissa Bentley that he found troubling. He sensed a barely concealed resentment, a bristling hostility just beneath a seductively attractive surface.

"Welcome back, Father, it's so nice to have you with us again. I look forward to your annual visit." Mark turned to see an old friend.

"No more than I do, Rita." The priest responded, taking her hand. "How have you been?"

"Just fine, Father. Of course we still miss Dad, but we are so grateful that you were here last year when he passed on. You were so helpful."

"I'm glad I was here at the right time, Rita. Your father was a very special man. It was a privilege to know him," Mark answered.

"Thank you, Father. He was very fond of you, too."

After removing his vestments, Mark returned to the cottage. The answering machine was flashing red. He hit the message replay button and was greeted by a familiar voice.

"Hey, Padre, it's me, Tim. The warden said I deserved a twenty-four hour pass away from the asylum for good behavior. I'm on my way and should darken your doorstep sometime around noon. See you then."

The voice belonged to Lt. Tim Bryant. The "warden" was Mary, Tim's wife. Mark had met the Bryants in his role as chaplain to the Mission District Precinct of the San Francisco Police Force. He had shared many meals with Tim, Mary and their nine children at their refurbished Victorian in the Richmond District. They were one of the most extraordinary families that Mark had ever known.

Mary had told Mark years ago that when she and Tim married, they had made a promise to each other. No matter what the future held for them, they would always be guided by the question, "What is the loving thing to do?"

Being faithful to that philosophy had led them to adopt seven of their children. It was the "special" children that Mary and Tim had gone out of their way to adopt. Among their children were the crippled, the hearing impaired, the racially mixed and a baby with Downs Syndrome.

These children were cherished members of the Bryant family and under the umbrella of Tim and Mary's loving care, they flourished.

Tim had been educated by the Jesuits and Mary had worked for the San Francisco Ballet, so between the two of them their children were receiving the closest thing to a classical education possible. Lessons in voice, music, dance and foreign languages didn't come cheaply, so Tim worked two jobs. In addition to being a police lieutenant, he was also a lawyer whose work for the Church had involved him in a couple of high profile cases in the last few years.

Mark picked up his breviary and walked out into the sunlit garden to say his midday prayers. Mark seated himself on the chaise lounge and opened the book to the prayers of the day. As he crossed himself to begin, his attention was drawn away by a strange buzzing sound. He raised his eyes and found himself looking into the face of a ruby-throated hummingbird. Hovering just inches from his nose like a miniature helicopter, the tiny bird seemed as curious about Mark as he was about it.

Iridescent emerald feathers shimmered for an instant in the bright sunlight. Mark's gaze followed the hummingbird's course until it disappeared into the immensity of the blue sky. He tried to return to his prayers but couldn't focus.

Perhaps this wasn't such a good place to pray after all, he thought. Despite the explosion of color around him, he felt his spirit sinking. A heaviness came over him as his thoughts turned to Shelby Townsend and their conversation.

She had thought it providential when she saw him twice in the space of a few days. Perhaps the Divine Providence extended now to Tim Bryant's visit. As a San Francisco policeman, Tim was no stranger to cult activity. If things happened the way Shelby described them, then certainly intimidation and murder were matters for the police. Tim would be an invaluable ally.

His thoughts were interrupted by the sound of car wheels crunching across the gravel drive of the chaplain's compound. Just as he reached the garden gate, it opened from the other side.

"Up pops the devil!" beamed Tim Bryant, juggling an overnight bag in one hand and one of Mary's apple pies in the other.

"Truer words than you think," answered the priest. A puzzled look came over the policeman's face.

"I'll explain later," said Mark, taking the pie. They walked back to the cottage and Tim went directly to the guest room to deposit his bag. He had enjoyed Mark's hospitality here many times and was familiar with the house.

"Hungry?" asked Mark.

"Is the Pope Catholic?" the smiling Irishman answered.

"How about lunch at Nepenthe?"

"You're on."

They piled into Tim's 1980 Cadillac limousine and headed south toward Big Sur. One of Tim's clients owned a limo service and kept Tim supplied with used fleet cars every couple of years in lieu of payment for services rendered. With nine children, Mary and Tim felt that they were practical as well as stylish. They weren't the minivan type of family.

Nepenthe was a good hour's drive down the coast from Carmel. The Greek restaurant was one of Mark's favorites. Like an eagle's nest, it hung high upon the rocky cliffs above the foaming waters. The outdoor terrace offered a spectacular view of the Pacific. Arriving before two o'clock, they were able to order from the lunch menu on Sunday.

Mark ordered a turkey sandwich and a Greek salad of lettuce, marinated tomatoes, feta cheese and Mediterranean olives. Tim went for the mousaka. Over lunch, Mark related the strange events of the last few days.

"So, Tim, what do you think? The girl strikes me as absolutely sincere and genuinely scared out of her wits."

His friend seemed lost in thought as he gazed out to sea. "Well, Padre, you're as good a judge of character as I've ever known. If you think she's being straight with you, then I certainly wouldn't discount her story. From the legal standpoint though, I'm not sure how much can be done. I mean, what do we have here? A teenager with a fantastic story. The sheriff's department has ruled the teacher's death either a suicide or an accident, right? We haven't even seen the official report. Apparently there is no hard evidence for the police to suspect foul play. So what it would ultimately come down to is one kid's word against another's."

Mark asked, "What about the marks on Jeff's palms?"

"Hardly solid evidence of murder or conspiracy. Now mind you, I'm only speaking from the very narrow perspective of what is legally admissible. That doesn't mean to say that I'm not convinced that everything happened just the way this young woman said it did and that she may be in the gravest danger."

He continued, "As a lawyer, I know what will work in a courtroom and what won't. As a cop who's worked the streets of San Francisco for years, I've learned to trust my gut. I've seen and heard enough things that can't be put into a police report to know that there is more to reality than what can be found in the California Code of Justice. Did I ever tell you my Larry Watkins story?"

"I don't think so."

"This was several years ago. We brought him in for loitering. At first we thought he was just another street person. He had taken up residence in the alley behind the home of an old lady in the Sunset District. She called us, terrified, because every night for several days running, she had been awakened by the sounds of a violent quarrel coming from the alley below her window. She counted at least three or four different voices. But when she looked out her window, what really terrified the old gal was that all four voices were coming from our friend Larry Watkins, esquire. He was having one hell of a debate with himself."

Mark said, "Granted, the different voices make it more interesting, but the City's full of mentally ill vagrants talking to themselves."

"It gets better. When we got him down to the station to book him, he proceeded to start talking backwards. In Latin. This wasn't a memorized con job; there was nothing halting or uncertain in his speech. His responses to our questions were in absolutely fluent and flawless classical Latin.

It scared the you-know-what out of the booking officers. I've still got most of it on tape. Father Maloney at the seminary translated the whole thing for me. So tell me, where does a twenty-two year old high school drop out drug addict learn to speak fluent Ciceronian Latin? And backwards, at that? So you see, Padre, you don't have to make a believer out of me. I'm already on board. What is that passage from St. Paul about the Powers of Darkness?"

The priest answered, "It's in Ephesians, Chapter six: 'For our struggle is not with flesh and blood, but against the principalities, the powers, the rulers of this present darkness, the evil spirits in the region above'."

The priest looked out across the waves. The bright blue of the afternoon sky had gone gray as a distant fog bank loomed on the horizon. The warm sunny day had suddenly turned dark and ominous. Like a cold, wet hand, the sea breeze fluttered across the back of his neck causing him to shiver.

Chapter 7

They returned to Mark's house in time to enjoy the sunset and a relaxing drink in front of the fireplace. But before entering the house, the two friends stood outside for a few minutes, totally absorbed in the incredible show that Mother Nature was putting on. Mark never got tired of this event. Sunset along the Pacific Coast was God's palette, always a breathtaking display of color---from softest corals to deepest reds, with yellow, orange and purple splattering a canvas of blue green and white, setting the horizon on fire.

As the sun silently sank beneath the waves, they turned in unison, still not speaking, and entered the house. In the evening shadows, Mark noticed the blinking red light on the phone announcing a message. Walking across the room, he pushed the button and heard Mother Benedicta's voice.

"Sorry to bother you on Sunday, Father, but the Monterey Hospital called to inform you they have admitted an accident victim. Her name is Shelby Townsend and she has been asking for you."

An icy cold band of fear gripped his heart at the mention of Shelby's name. He looked at Tim and without a word they turned around and headed for the car.

Arriving at the hospital, they parked in emergency vehicle parking, thank's to Tim's 'Police' placard, and hurried into the emergency room.

"Good evening, Miss, I'm Father Ross. I understand you have a patient named Shelby Townsend here?"

"Not here, Father. She has been moved up to Room

312. She is doing fine. The doctor just wants to keep her overnight for observation."

"Thank God." Mark sighed with relief. "May we go up to her room?"

"Yes, of course, Father, just take the main elevators up to three and check with the floor-charge nurse. Miss Townsend kept asking for you. It seemed very important that she speak with you."

"Thanks," Mark said as he turned to the elevators. "Tim," he said almost under his breath, "are you thinking what I am?"

"Let's not jump to any conclusions, Padre," Tim warned. "This could be just what they said it was---an accident. Hell, you know how some teenagers are behind the wheel."

"I told you how mature this girl seems to be," Mark reminded him. The elevator door slid back and they stepped in. They rode up in silence, stepped out on the third floor and approached the nurses' station.

"Good evening, Miss Jenkins," Mark spoke, taking advantage of her name badge. "I'm Father Ross and this is Lieutenant Bryant. I wonder if we might visit Miss Townsend in Room 312?"

"Oh, Father, I'm glad you're here," the nurse replied. "She's been in quite a state. For some reason she is very worried about you. Her parents just left to get a bite of dinner but I know Shelby is awake and waiting for you. Her room is just down the hall to the left."

"Thank you, Miss Jenkins. We'll try not to stay too late."

Tim entered the small room behind Mark. Both men tried to conceal their surprise when they looked down at the battered and bruised girl. Stitches were over her blackened left eye and a deep purple bruise was already beginning to form over the left cheek bone making her look like a mugging victim. Her left arm was in a splint and sling. Mark assumed it was not broken, merely sprained.

"Someone wasn't wearing her seat belt." Tim grinned as he spoke.

Shelby looked confused.

"This is my good friend, Lt. Tim Bryant of the San Francisco Police," Mark introduced him. "And, Tim, I'd like you to meet Miss Shelby Townsend." Shelby tried to smile but couldn't. Her lower lip trembled and tear drops squeezed between her closed eyelids.

"Don't worry, Shelby, I'm not here to give you a traffic ticket. I'm just tagging along with Father Mark."

This time, Tim's sense of humor got a tiny smile from the girl. She looked up at Mark with frightened eyes. "Are you all right, Father?"

"Yes, Shelby, I'm fine, but what about you?" Mark asked with real concern. "What happened?"

"Father, they know I told you. I'm sure that this was a warning to me."

"You can't mean that someone deliberately caused your accident?"

"My brakes were in perfect condition. And on my way to work this afternoon, they just weren't there when I stepped on them." She glanced at Tim.

"Did you tell him, Father?" she asked defensively.

"Yes. Lt. Bryant has a great deal of experience with this sort of thing. I told him in the hope that he could help us."

"Shelby, I would like to help if I may," Tim added.

"Well, I guess it's ok, since Father has already told you." she agreed.

"Good, let's begin with the accident. What makes you think it was a deliberate act on someone's part?"

"I don't think, I know." A defensive tone overshadowed her voice. "I went to Miss Wayland and look what happened to her. And now you're in danger, too." She began to cry, looking up at the concerned men standing at her bedside. "I'm so sorry," she whispered.

"Shelby, Miss Wayland's death was an accident," Mark said calmly. "It was just a coincidence that she drowned and that you had an accident."

"No, Father, it's all my fault. I never should have gone to her for help. And I never should have involved you, either. Now you are in danger and so is your friend." She tried to roll over to bury her face in her pillow.

"Did you notice if anyone was following you this afternoon, Shelby?" Tim again interrupted.

"I didn't see anyone. But I know they were there."

"How do you know that? Perhaps your brakes were wet," Tim reasoned.

"No, there was nothing wrong with them. I know," she insisted.

Mark and Tim both turned as they heard footsteps coming down the hall.

"It's my Mom and Dad." Shelby tried to sit up. "Don't tell them about this, please," she begged.

Anne and Michael Townsend stepped into the room and hesitated when they saw the two men.

"Mom, Dad, this is my friend Father Mark Ross from the monastery, and his friend, Tim Bryant," Shelby said carefully not to reveal what Tim's line of work was.

"Father, Tim, these are my folks, Michael and Anne Townsend."

"How do you do, Father, Mr. Bryant." Michael Townsend's voice was courteous, if not friendly. "How is it you know my daughter, Father? I don't recall her ever mentioning your name."

Shelby jumped in, "I've been thinking of going back to Church, Dad, and Father Ross has been kind enough to help me."

"Oh? Why didn't you discuss this with your father and me?" Anne Townsend interrupted.

"I wasn't sure how you and Dad would feel about it. And anyway, Mom, I was just thinking about it," Shelby offered.

"Is that why you were so insistent about seeing a priest?" Anne Townsend seemed almost relieved.

"Yes, Mom, I didn't want him to worry about why I didn't show up after work."

Mark recognized Shelby's excuse as a lie, but it seemed to be accepted by her parents. "Well, Shelby, I think you need some rest now. Why don't I come back tomorrow? That is, if it's all right with you." He looked to the parents as he turned to take his leave.

"Of course, Father," Anne Townsend answered.

"I'm sorry we had to meet under such circumstances." Mark reached out to shake hands with Michael.

"Good-bye Shelby, Mrs. Townsend. It was nice meeting you." Tim gave Anne his best smile and winked at Shelby.

Michael followed Tim and Mark into the hall. "Excuse me, Father, but how long has Shelby been seeing you?"

"Actually, we just met yesterday. She was my waitress at the Club. We got to talking and she asked if she could see me at the monastery after work," Mark admitted.

"Oh, I had hoped that perhaps she had been seeing you longer. She has been troubled about something for weeks now. She just hasn't been herself lately. Her mother and I have been very worried about her. That's probably why she ran off the road today---thinking about something and not paying attention to her driving. She insisted it was her brakes, but I had that car checked out from top to bottom before I let her buy it. I know those brakes were all right. But to be sure, I'm going to have our mechanic look at them tomorrow."

"That's a good idea, Mr. Townsend. Perhaps you'd give the good Father a call to let him know about the brakes," Tim broke in.

"I will. Thank you both for coming. I know it was important to Shelby. Perhaps she'll be able to get some sleep now. I know her grandmother will be happy to learn that at least one of us is getting back to the Church."

Tim had said very little throughout the visit, but Mark knew he had missed nothing. They walked in silence back to the parking lot, each in his own thoughts.

"Do you think there is something to worry about, Tim?"

"Well, I'm not saying anything just yet, but it doesn't hurt to cover all possibilities. I'd like to get a look at the car first thing tomorrow morning before I go back up to the City."

****

The bank of candles burning in front of the statues of the Madonna and Child flickered in unison. Like tiny ballerinas, the golden flames swayed and danced as if moved by a breeze, but the aged nun kneeling there in the deserted chapel hadn't felt any draft.

Ordinarily Mother Benedicta treasured these quiet moments. She smiled when she thought of the stereotypes with which the world approached cloistered religious life--- Hollywood images of beautiful ladies floating serenely through polished corridors of mahogany and marble, untouched and untroubled by the unruly passions of the human heart or the chaos of the world outside. It seemed a lifetime ago that she had shared these sugar-coated cliches.

But forty years behind monastery walls had long since disabused her of such pious platitudes. Life in a monastery was a life of constant struggle, a life of busy routines in which every moment was measured out and accounted for.

Like a pendulum, the hours of the day swung between the two poles of communal prayer and physical labor and she hungered for these moments alone with her God. As the superior, she had the additional burdens of administration in this thriving community.

Long after the rest of the community had retired, a solitary lamp could often be seen burning in the window of Mother Superior's corner office. Tonight, however, the only light emanating from the monastery was the pulsating indigo of stained glass illuminated from within by a hundred flickering candles.

Tonight the old nun's heart was heavy. Her interior peace of soul was troubled by the disturbing conversation she had had with Father Mark Ross a few hours ago. She tried to imagine Shelby Townsend, thinking perhaps she was one of those bright and pretty youngsters who had come to visit the monastery in years past on field trips with her schoolmates.

In her mind's eye she could still see their faces, eyes shining with wonder and curiosity looking back at her from the other side of the grille. It had been a long time now since any class had been permitted to come for a visit. She remembered these beautiful young faces and her heart ached for their stolen innocence.

The sisters were prayer warriors who had dedicated their lives to fighting for good on a supernatural level. A lifetime of prayer and contemplation had left her with a sensitivity to the shifting tides of spiritual warfare. She was more aware of the unseen forces vying with each other in realms of light and shadow, having witnessed their contest on the battlefield of her own soul.

She had become experienced in detecting in others that lightness of spirit which indicated the presence of grace or the clammy, putrid rot that seemed to suck the life force from the vital centers of the living---the unmistakable mark of the Beast.

Tonight, the scent of brimstone seemed to lay heavy in the air. What the young priest had learned from books, she had learned from experience. What he had learned in the classroom, she had learned on the battlefield. She had seen the rough and ragged Beast grow bolder.

Like sentinels, Mother Benedicta and many like her had stood their posts on invisible spiritual battlements and held the line.   Humanity's faith in God had been the supernatural barricade that had held the Beast in check, but as mankind had abandoned God, that wall of light and love had begun to crumble.   It was now so weak, so thin and stretched, that the Beast could punch holes through it.   And through the breech poured a tide so black and foul that it threatened to plunge the whole world into eternal night.

The innocence of the young was among the first casualties.   Her heart went out to them tonight in prayer.   All around her she could feel the powers of good and evil gathering, preparing to take the contest to a new level in this particular corner of the vineyard.

The battleground might shift, but the struggle was always the same one.   The tension in the air could be felt.   There was a sharpness to light and sound, a tautness like a violin string stretched to the point of snapping.

Armies were preparing for battle.   She had felt it approaching for weeks.   For days she had been awakened suddenly out of a sound sleep at precisely three o'clock in the morning.   From past experience she knew that it meant the enemy was up to something.

There was an old saying that no one believes in God like the devil.   The Beast was obsessed by hatred of the All Holy One.   He could only mock what he himself could never be.   As it was at three p.m. that Christ accomplished His work of Redemption giving up His spirit on the cross, so it was at three a.m. that the devil sent out his legions to do their worst.   Everything that God did, the devil tried to undo.   Where God had given life, the devil gave death. Where God had given innocence, the devil gave corruption.

The immortal souls of these children were at stake. Mother Benedicta knew her part in the battle for their souls was an invisible one. She could only pray that her fasting, midnight vigils and sacrifices would generate the spiritual energy needed to tip the scales in their favor.

Salvation was God's work. But he did give human beings a role to play in the great conflict between good and evil. And according to God's mysterious economy, human effort mattered. Free will was no mere fiction. The good that people strove for and the evil that they did made a difference in time and eternity.

Mother Benedicta's faith assured her that in the long run, God's will would triumph. In the short run, however, evil could and often did win unless the forces of goodness were very, very careful. And even when goodness did win, it was usually at a terrible cost. She raised her eyes to the crucifix above the altar.

The unseen, unfelt breeze moved through the darkened chapel and caused the candles to flicker again. It was as though a vacuum had occurred, caused by a portal opening between two worlds. The old nun's lips moved in silent prayer, "Forgive us our trespasses as we forgive those who trespass against us. And lead us not into temptation, but deliver us from the Evil One."

****

In another part of town, a sudden gust of wind rushed through the dry, dead leaves that still clung to the California Oak outside Chloe's bedroom window, creating a sound like aluminum foil being crinkled. Always a light sleeper, she was instantly awake and alert. Chloe lay there listening to the sounds of the night, wondering what had awakened her.

She listened to the chirping insects, the gentle tinkling of wind chimes, rustling trees. She identified each one as it passed across her consciousness. They should have been familiar, comforting sounds, but something seemed wrong.

There was something else in the mix, like a sour note in a symphony that was jarring and out of place. Something that didn't fit.

There it was again. A sharp clacking noise that accompanied each new gust of wind. Taking a flashlight, she pulled her robe on and padded silently through the dark house.

As she neared the patio doors leading out to the garden, the noise grew louder and more demanding. She was slowly turning the handles of the French doors just as another gust of wind wrenched them from her grip and flung them open, almost causing her to lose her balance.

Chloe looked out across the flagstone patio to see the origin of the annoying sound. The open door of her dove coop was swinging back and forth, banging against the frame. The pen was empty. She tied the door open so that it would stop banging. Perhaps some of the birds would find their way home.

Chapter 8

The first fingers of daylight were beginning to probe the grayness of the pre-dawn sky as Tim waved a final farewell. As his friend turned up the Coast Highway toward San Francisco, Mark headed over to the chapel to begin his spiritual preparation for Mass.

The early hours of the morning just before dawn were his ideal time for prayer. Spiritual senses seemed sharper in those early hours when light and darkness battled for supremacy. The world seemed to hold a collective breath in that moment of perfect balance between light and darkness.

As he watched the sun come up over the horizon from the front steps of the chapel, he thought of the philosopher Goethe's dying words---"Mehr licht!" "More light!" More light indeed. He would need more light if he were going to be able to help Shelby Townsend. The time had come for some serious research.

After Mass, he made his excuses to the Breakfast Club and instead accepted a rain check for dinner at Chloe's home that evening. Turning Angus loose in the safety of the garden courtyard, he drove into the village to begin his search for knowledge at "The Book Worm".

Entering the bookstore from Ocean Avenue, Mark descended a steep set of stairs that took him below the street. Despite its subterranean status, the store was surprisingly bright and cheerful.

What disturbed him about most popular bookstore chains in California was that the section on New Age and Occult books was almost always at lease two or three times larger than the section on Religion or Philosophy.

And what was true for the literary set also seemed true for the general public. Mark had often noted that invariably the largest section of any neighborhood video store were the horror films. As a priest, it especially galled him to see Bibles and books on religion mixed with books on spirit channeling and divination. He couldn't help but wonder if the New Age movement had gained credibility in the popular mind or if religion had degenerated to the level of just another superstition as far as American culture was concerned.

His search at the bookstore yielded nothing of value, just the inevitable New Age fluff that combined pop-psychology with Oriental mysticism suitably watered down for American palates. His next stop would be the Carmel Public Library.

Like many of the public buildings on the Monterey peninsula, the library was done in the Spanish Revival style of the 1920's. Here he fared better. His search yielded "A Guide to Grand Jury Men with Respect to Witches and Demonianism" and even a translation of the "Malleus Maleficarum".

Waiting at the counter to check out his finds, Mark's attention wandered over to the public bulletin board by the exit. Amid the chaos of handbills and index cards stapled to the kiosk was something that immediately caught his eye.

On an 8 ½ by 11 piece of pink copy paper was the same symbol he had seen around Marissa Bentley's neck yesterday, a triangle with a cross at each point. Gathering up his books, he walked over to the bulletin board to take a closer look.

As he approached, the words beneath the symbol came into focus: "Discover the Goddess and God within. Learn to tap into your own divine energy. Meditation classes at the Crystal Visions Bookstore every Friday at eight p.m. All those sincerely seeking higher consciousness are welcome."

Mark pulled the embossed business card from his wallet and wasn't surprised that it matched the flyer on the board in front of him. "Marissa Bentley. I should have known," he said to himself. "I think it's about time I got a little 'higher consciousness' myself." He pushed his way through the double doors into the bright California sunshine.

Crystal Visions was located in one of those quaint, cottage-like buildings that made up so much of downtown Carmel. Mark found it in a courtyard off a narrow, shaded side street flanked by a coffee shop and an art gallery.

The uneven flagstones, buckled by the root system of an ancient pine, were a hazard to navigate and the priest nearly stumbled as he approached the shop. Behind the latticed glass of a large display window was an assortment of crystal balls, tarot cards and pewter dragons and wizards. Entering the shop, he was immediately assailed by the pungent fragrance of sandlewood incense wafting in his direction from behind a curtain of beaded cords that separated the store from a room in the back. A tape of what sounded like Tibetan Monks chanting, was playing.

Mark glanced over the shelves, surprised to see St. Teresa of Avila's "Interior Castle", a classic of Christian spirituality, next to "The Tibetan Book of the Dead". There were bags of rune stones next to rosaries and Ouija Boards next to Bibles. It all seemed jumbled and confused without rhyme or reason.

As he continued to browse he came across some works that he was unhappily familiar with---"The Book of Shadows" by Gerald Brousseau Gardinier, "The Black Arts" by Richard Cavendish and some demented poetry by Aleister Crowley. He had encountered these authors while writing a term paper on the Black Mass during his college days.

The name of Aleister Crowley in particular brought with it a wave of revulsion. The most famous self-proclaimed sorcerer of the Twentieth Century used to sign his letters "The Beast."

Crowley had risen through the ranks of the European occult hierarchy to eventually become the Master of the Order of Templars of the Orient. The story was circulated throughout secret societies at the turn of the century that Crowley commanded an army of forty-nine demons and had killed his rivals by means of black magic.

The curtain of plastic beads rattled as it parted and Mark looked up to see Marissa Bentley emerge from the back room. Again she was dressed in black, and Mark could not help but compare her to a sleek black cat.

"I thought I felt a disturbance in the Force," she said in reference to "Star Wars", greeting the priest with a broad smile.

"Hardly Darth Vader, just your friendly neighborhood priest. But if I had to identify with someone from your 'Star Wars' analogy, I'd have to pick Obi Wan Kenobi."

"Looking for Luke Skywalker then, or here to perform an exorcism?"

"Neither. Like the sign says, I'm searching for a little 'higher consciousness' and you seem to be in the enlightenment business." He looked around the room. "Besides, I thought I'd been invited."

"Let's just say I'm a friendly competitor," Marissa retorted.

Their banter seemed easygoing, almost friendly, but the atmosphere was suddenly charged with growing tension. The beautiful woman nervously fondled the medallion about her neck.

"Somehow, I don't think we're selling the same thing," said the priest, holding up a copy of Aleister Crowley's poems. "There is nothing enlightening or uplifting about this. In fact, it's the kind of soul-corrupting poison that is landing a lot of people, especially young people, in hell."

"I'm surprised that you are familiar with the works of Aleister Crowley. I must say, I'm impressed." Her whole demeanor was one of smug superiority.

"It's always best to know one's enemy," the priest retorted.

"We seem to be having the same conversation. Once again, Father, that is your opinion. Fortunately for those with open minds, the Constitution allows a variety of expressions in the search for spirituality."

"Oh, I believe in being open-minded, Marissa, but not so open-minded that your brain falls out. When you can no longer distinguish between good and evil, between what elevates the human spirit and what degrades it, then you haven't merely lost sight of the truth, you've forgotten what it looks like."

"Good and evil, pain and pleasure, life and death, light and darkness---aren't they all just different sides of the same coin?" she argued. "After all, don't they need each other to define themselves? You can't really have God without the Devil, can you?"

"That's been argued to death, Marissa. It's just so much New Age superstition."

"What you call superstition, I call ancient wisdom. The time has come for women to re-claim their own power. The Church with its male hierarchy will never help them do that. All through history, the Church has held women in bondage, canonizing cultural patriarchy as if it were divinely inspired."

She went on, "Even your God is a man. How can you blame us for looking to a wisdom that pre-dates Christianity in our search for our own power? It's time for all who are oppressed to break our chains and become strong and independent. In my own way, I try to help people---especially women---find that freedom. That's what places like this are all about---enlightenment. Helping people to find the God within themselves."

"Somehow, Marissa, when you say helping people find the God within, what I really think you mean is telling people they are God."

"Semantics, Father Ross. It's just a question of how you use the word."

"Semantics? I'd call it idolatry. Isn't that what so much New Age philosophy comes down to? Deciding for yourself what's right and wrong, good and evil, making your own will the absolute moral norm? Sounds pretty convenient to me. After all, if I am God, then who is there to tell me I must obey? If I am God, what possible ethical prohibitions apply to me any longer? Who can be my judge if I get to create my own reality as I go along? Call it New Age, there's nothing new about it at all. It's as old as the Garden of Eden."

Just then the door latch clicked open and Mark turned around in time to see a young girl step in from the courtyard. From the pile of high school textbooks under her arm, Mark assumed she must be a teenager, and yet her appearance was made older by a disquieting detail.

From head to foot, she was dressed entirely in black. Seeing the priest in his Roman collar, the young woman froze in her tracks. Her eyes shone with an expression of paralyzed fear as she looked helplessly back and forth from Mark to Marissa.

Realizing that the opportunity to make a graceful retreat had passed, she forced herself into the room and positioned herself along the wall with her back to the priest, pretending to be absorbed in the first book she could bury her face in.

Marissa's body stiffened under the force of her icy will as she struggled to maintain her casual façade. Mark sensed some unspoken communication passing between them. Suddenly, she was all business.

"So what will it be, Father Ross, something to keep you awake or something to put you to sleep?"

"Neither. I think I've found what I was looking for.

A hint of frost edged her words. "Sorry I couldn't be of help to you, but do feel free to come back and browse anytime."

With those parting words, she abruptly turned and retreated behind the beaded curtain. Mark heard the front door close softly behind him and he suddenly found himself all alone again with the incense and chanting Lamas.

****

Chloe Martin's renovated farm house was about six miles from the village along the Carmel Valley Road. Mark reached it just seconds ahead of the fog, which moved inland like an advancing army, rolling over everything in its path. Mother Nature blanketed the golden hills and gnarled oak groves in a soft comforter of billowing gray mist.

Chloe met him at the door with an old-fashioned in one hand and an apron in the other. Thrusting them both in his direction, she said, "You're just in time, Mark, come in. You can help with the salad." She looked out into her garden at the fog rolling in. "Boy it looks like it's going to be a real pea-souper tonight."

The hardwood floor creaked beneath Mark's feet as he followed her through the house. He had always loved this old house, which was as much a product of Chloe's artistic ability as anything she had ever put on canvas. The open beamed ceiling, Shaker furnishing and walnut bookcases combined to produce an effect of relaxed formality that Mark often referred to as "elegant California casual."

The first impression one got was one of homey comfort. But a closer look revealed a studied casualness: from the four blue peacock feathers carefully arranged on an ochre tray on the coffee table, to the cream-colored border of the area rug which perfectly matched the flagstone fireplace.

Nothing had been added to the room without thought to form, color or balance. Harmony like this didn't just happen by accident. Normally the floor to ceiling windows and French doors would have flooded the room with sunshine, creating a light and airy feeling. But this evening, the swirling mist enveloping the house, coupled with the crackling fireplace created an atmosphere that was the essence of warmth and coziness.

A wonderful, mouth-watering aroma hung in the air as he entered the large country kitchen. There was something familiar in the exotic mix of spices that he couldn't quite put his finger on.

"What's for dinner?"

"I'm trying out one of my new recipes on you tonight. Chicken New Orleans. You're going to be my guinea pig."

"All in all, Chloe, I suppose I'd rather be a guinea pig than someone's pigeon."

"Did I miss something?" she asked, giving him a quizzical look over the top of her rhinestone-studded glasses. Slipping the apron over his head, Mark walked over to the butcher's block in the center of the kitchen and started slicing tomatoes.

"Remember the conversation we had in the Little Swiss Café my first morning here? You, Paul and Agatha were filling me in on some of the strange things that have been happening down here this year."

"Sure. Why?"

"Well, since then I've gotten closer than you can imagine to this whole ugly business. In fact, even you yourself may be closer to it than you think. It all begins with a young girl you may know. Her name is Shelby Townsend. It also involves your friend Janet Wayland."

He had her total attention now. "Dinner can wait," she said as she turned the oven to low. "Let's go into the living room."

Chloe freshened Mark's drink, refilled her own glass of Chablis and settled down next to Mark in front of the fire. As Mark unfolded his story, the furrows in Chloe's brow deepened and her expression became more intense. At the mention of Marissa Bentley, Chloe arched her eyebrows and nodded.

"I've run into the mysterious Ms. Bentley before, at the high school. She was invited as a guest speaker to one of the student assemblies to give a demonstration on Eastern Meditation. Needless to say, it was heavily laced with a generous portion of New Age philosophy that just bordered on an open endorsement of the occult. But she's a clever one. She knew just how far she could go and then let innuendo do the rest."

"That's the insidiousness of it all," said Mark with sudden anger. "The fascination with the occult can often begin with these meditative techniques. At first they're presented to people merely as simple non-sectarian, relaxation exercises. But just scratch the surface and you'll find that they carry with them an implicit presupposition about God and the human person that are anything but philosophically neutral. Yet, at the same time, the academic establishment has a fear of organized religion, particularly Christianity, that borders on the paranoid."

Chloe nodded her head in agreement. "I saw it at Berkeley and I've seen it here. I understand that the new principal has put a stop to the custom of taking class field trips to the monastery on Career Day, all in the name of the separation of church and state."

"But why don't they see that these methods of meditation are just as much based upon a philosophy and an anthropology, as any religion?" Mark asked.

"People see what they want to see. Academics are no more immune to bias than anyone else." Chloe got up and went over to the bookcases that lined an entire wall of the room. "Describe that medallion of Marissa Bentley's again," she requested.

"I've got a picture of it right here on her business card." Retrieving the card from his wallet, he handed it to her.

Holding the card in one hand, Chloe ran her free one over the books as she made her way along the shelves. Finding the one she was searching for, she pulled it out from the shelf and sat down again next to Mark in front of the fire. Rifling through the pages, she seemed to know what she was looking for.

"Isn't that the text you assigned us in your 'Art in Archaeology' course back at Berkeley?"

"The very same," she answered. "Ahha, here it is. I thought this thing reminded me of something." She handed the book to Mark. He took it and placed it in his lap.

In the reflected glow of the fire, he found himself looking again at the same symbol carved in stone. But in the circle that surrounded the pyramid were signs of the zodiac intermingled with the following names: Adonai, Tetragrammaton and Elohim.

The caption below the photograph identified it as an inscription carved into a castle wall reputed to have been a stronghold of the Order of the Knights Templar.

"The Knights Templar?" said Mark. "I've heard the name before, but I know almost nothing about them."

"They were a Twelfth Century order of Crusader Knights, the first and most powerful of the military orders. The Templars were the terror of the Moslem world. In two hundred years they had acquired such vast wealth that their power rivaled that of the King of France who launched his own crusade against them."

She continued explaining, "Philip IV of France was able to enlist the help of the Pope against the Knights by accusing them of sacrilege and witchcraft. The Order was dissolved by the Pope in 1312 and their Grand Master, along with many of the Knights, were burned alive at the stake. But the rumor persisted for centuries that they were merely driven underground. Whether or not they were really practicing the black arts or were falsely accused has been a matter of scholarly debate for a hundred years."

The wind had picked up outside and the French doors suddenly shuddered with a violence that startled Mark. It caused him to lose his grip on the book, which fell to the floor with a clap.

He looked toward the windows. Only a thin pane of glass separated their warm and cozy world from the swirling, clammy mist beyond. In his imagination, the billowing fog creeping into the garden was transformed into thick plumes of gray smoke.

The briny scent of the sea breeze mingled with the acrid stench of fire. The logs in the fireplace hissed with the agonized screams and dying curses of the doomed

Knights. In radiant embers, like the golden glow of cat's eyes, the devouring flames molded each crusader into a shrieking pillar of fire.

****

The wooden match scraped along the box and burst into a hissing flame like a tiny sparkler on the Fourth of July. For the briefest moment, the pervasive blackness of the room was beaten back by a pinpoint of light.

The flame flared bravely and then began to fade. A second before the darkness overwhelmed it, a trembling hand held it to the black candles that adorned the makeshift altar.

The young woman was dressed entirely in black and in the eerie glow she appeared to be a disembodied head floating in the void.

Her hand trembled in anticipation. She was becoming more and more adept at "the craft." Each time she practiced, she felt the Powers drawing closer. Soon she would be ready for his embrace---she felt certain of it.

She could feel his presence, sense his power gathering around her more and more, and she thrilled at his nearness. Tonight at the abandoned house she had felt him all around her, waiting for her. She could hardly wait to leave those adolescent amateurs and to return home to her room. She was certain that tonight would be the night she had been waiting for.

When she looked at her companions at school, she recognized them now for what they were---sheep. It seemed incredible to her now that she had ever envied them, ever wanted to be like them, ever given them the power to hurt her. She remembered how it had hurt her to be labeled a freak by the strong and beautiful ones.

She had all the power now and would make them pay. When she became strong enough, he would show her how. She delighted in imagining it. How many times each day would she rehearse in her mind her favorite scenarios: a broken leg for him, a scarred and mutilated face for her and so on. Her list was long---long enough to embrace a former friend or two.

Even her parents would learn of her power. Why should they be spared? They never had time for her. The only thing they ever thought of was their next high, their next drink. They had never been there when she had cried herself to sleep night after night. "Just sit down and watch your video and be quiet," had been the theme song of her childhood.

Sitting in the center of the pentagram, she was surrounded by a circle of burning black candles---a Black Widow enfolded in the heart of her web, waiting for her prey. She began chanting as her teacher had taught her, calling upon the Powers of Darkness. She closed her eyes and opened her soul to the dark communion she hungered for.

"Master, come. Come and do your servant's bidding." She had chanted the command hundreds of times before. This time the invitation was accepted. An unseen energy began to pour into the room like a slithering mist seeping in under the door and tumbling over the transom.

The warm velvet blackness started to coil itself like a serpent around the consciousness of the young woman. A powerful psychic force began applying pressure to a certain part of her brain, blocking the flight response and supressing her human instincts of self-preservation.

Only for the briefest second did she feel the faintest flicker of fear, like someone unable to catch his breath, before it was quickly snuffed out. The room started to spin around her like some crazy carousel and she had a feeling of weightlessness. It was euphoric. She felt peacefully detached from her surroundings, detached from her anxieties, detached from herself.

Her anger, her pain, her fear no longer existed. There was only the warm darkness, the floating and the strange tingling feeling. Time and space, yesterday and tomorrow, were displaced in this all-encompassing dimension of perfect tranquillity. She would have done anything to hold on to this high. Nothing mattered but this. Nothing but this.

A door in her mind was being slowly, gently pried open. When her token, instinctual resistance had been stroked into dreamy surrender, the great black tide surged forward, approaching as from a far-off distance, but moving with breath-taking speed, eager to take possession.

The whirring, rushing sound approaching was like a cyclone bearing down on her, roaring through her head. A suffocating weight pressed in on her from all sides. She felt as if she were being crushed, like some deep-sea diver falling helplessly into the oblivion of a bottomless abyss.

From some faraway place deep in her soul, she heard a strange, pitiful noise. Reedy and high-pitched, only gradually did it dawn upon her that she was listening to the sound of screams---her own---shrieking like a train whistle as it hurled through the night.

Suddenly everything around her blazed with color. An exploding rainbow of iridescent hues filled the night as the terrible coldness seared through her with the intensity of a million suns, penetrating the depths of her crumbling soul.

Whatever feeble resistance she could have offered was contemptuously brushed aside by the force that had ripped the child's mind from its hinges. All that was left of Stacy Ballard's self-consciousness was rapidly dissolving under the all-devouring appetite of a fiend who fed off the spiritual essence of other beings.

In clawed black hands, it held her soul, regarding her with rapacious red eyes as a bird of prey would a mouse caught in its bloody talons. She surrendered to that hideous strength. What remained of Stacy Ballard flickered for an instant, like a smoldering wick, then faded into oblivion. When her eyes opened, what beheld the world from behind them was something else.

Chapter 9

Mark's headlights pierced through the blackness as he drove up the long drive to the monastery. Occasionally the moon sailed clear of the heavy cloud cover and he was able to make out black shapes that during the day were beautiful trees and rock formations. But on a night like this, they were just dark hulks and pillars that inflamed the phantoms of his imagination. Get hold of yourself, he thought.

He stopped the car at the top of the drive, knowing that the monastery gates would be locked after nine p.m. In the light of his high beams, Mark found the keypad on the gate post and punched in the numerical code.

The gates clicked and began to swing open as he hurried back to the car, knowing that they would return to their locked position almost immediately.

He couldn't explain why, but he felt a sense of relief hearing the gates as they slid back into place. He even lingered for a few seconds, looking into his rear-view mirror at the massive gates just to satisfy himself that nothing had sneaked in behind him.

He was already in the carport when he thought he heard the electric hum of the gates sliding open again. My imagination, he thought.

Stepping out of the car, he realized that it was much darker in the garden than it should have been. Mark knew he had left the light on above the statue of Mary just outside the garden gate.

"What a night for the light bulb to burn out," he grumbled, fumbling for his house key as he inched his way across the dark garden.

"Ouch!" He stumbled and almost fell over a wooden bench that should have been out by the lemon tree. Pain flashed from his shin like a lightning bolt. How did that blasted bench get over here? he wondered. Angus began barking furiously inside the house.

"Quiet, boy. It's me. Stop that infernal racket or you'll wake up the sisters." Angus continued barking. Mark stepped gingerly across the garden, one hand feeling his way along the side of the house, the other stretched out in front of him like a blind man searching for the door.

"Damn." A night like this gave new meaning to the word dark. Why hadn't he left the blasted light on? He could have sworn he had.

Just then the clouds parted, allowing enough moonlight for him to make his way across the courtyard to the door. Before the moon slid behind another cloud, Mark found the keyhole and unlocked the door. Stumbling over the welcome mat, he heard the distinctive sound of glass crunch beneath the soles of his shoes.

He opened the door and reached inside, running his fingers over the wall, looking for the light switch. He switched the first button up and down, but the outside remained dark. He moved his fingers on to the next button and switched on the overhead hallway light.

Golden light flooded the hall and spilled outside to illuminate some of the garden courtyard. He could see the broken glass of the shattered light bulb everywhere on the path, near both the doorway and the carport. This was no accident, this was a deliberate act of vandalism. He was relieved that he hadn't left Angus outside in the courtyard tonight.

"Here, Angus. Here, boy…" Mark called his friend. The dog came bounding out from his hiding place under Mark's bed.

"Poor old man," Mark crooned to the dog as he rubbed his ears. "What happened here tonight? Looks like you had quite a scare."

Angus growled. A deep, throaty rumbling that almost sounded intelligible. He wanted desperately to share something with his master.

Mark tried to calm his friend. "Well, don't worry, fella, whoever it was is gone. We're okay." Carefully walking through the house, checking the rooms for signs of entry or more vandalism, Mark was finally satisfied that his visitors had not gotten inside the house. Angus scratched impatiently at the front door.

"Come along, Angus, better use the backyard tonight. Too much glass in the courtyard for your paws. Besides, we need to check this side of the house."

He slipped Angus's leash on his collar. Normally, Angus would stay with him on his night walks, but tonight Mark wasn't taking any chances. Angus was very territorial and always ready to challenge any interlopers.

Mark's secretary always felt completely safe when she had Angus in the office. She laughed that his bark was mightier than his size. No one gained entrance without Angus's permission.

With flashlight in one hand and Angus's leash in the other, Mark checked the grounds around the house. It was clear that someone had deliberately broken the outside lights and frightened Angus, but Mark could see no other signs of vandalism.

Just some pre-Halloween pranksters having a little fun at Father's expense, he thought. On the other hand, it could be more serious. After all, Angus was completely black and too many small black animals disappeared around this time of year, ending up as ritual sacrifices.

"Come along, Angus, let's get back to the house. It's getting cold out here." They turned around and walked towards the warm glow of light pouring over the patio through the open French doors.

Once inside, Mark drew the drapes, put a match to the waiting Duraflame log in the fireplace and poured himself a bedtime brandy. Retrieving a book from his bedside table, he settled down to enjoy the fire and unwind a bit before bed.

The warmth radiating from the fireplace and the brandy began to do their work and Mark began to relax. With the gates securely locked and the drapes drawn, the room became a snug cocoon for the two old friends. They began to doze, Angus resting his head on Mark's lap.

The priest was floating in a dreamy no man's land between sleep and consciousness when something suddenly dragged him back to the surface. He sat up, totally alert, awake and waiting.

Angus sprang up. The dog stood stone still, like a statue. Every muscle tensed and ready. Ears up and turning like radar dishes. His low rumbling growl broke the silence of the room.

"What is it , boy? What do you hear?" There it was again---the unmistakable sound of someone walking on the roof. Mark was sure of it. It was so distinct that he could even chart its progress across the ceiling.

Angus let loose with a barrage of barking. Mark's heart was pounding. It felt as though it was pushing against the muscles at the base of his throat, trying to break free of the confinement of his chest. He inhaled deeply, trying to pull himself together.

"Stay, Angus!" he ordered. Grabbing a flashlight from the kitchen, he raced out the front door. Standing in the middle of the courtyard, he pointed the shaft of light up to the roof.

The beam of light caught something moving along the roof line. Two red eyes glared back at him. Suddenly the dark form leaped from the roof into the branches of a small lemon tree. Mark realized he had been holding his breath as it rushed out of him with enough force to make him dizzy. His attention was riveted to the lemon tree as he watched a large raccoon scurry down and race away into the night.

Mark retreated just as quickly to the warmth of the fireplace. Grateful that there was no one there to see his red face, he was almost too embarrassed to look at Angus.

"Come on, boy, we'd best get to bed. We've had enough for one night. Sure glad you can't talk. I'd hate to have you tell anyone about our night stalker." Mark leaned over the fireplace to secure the screen. It won't do to start another California fire, he thought.

Tonight Angus was welcome to sleep on the foot of the bed. Somehow, another warm body, another heartbeat was a source of comfort to both man and beast. After the adrenalin rush subsided, a sense of fatigue pressed down upon him and his eyes grew heavy. It seemed like only a few minutes before Mark was awakened by the sound of

Angus's low growling. Mark looked at the glowing green numerals on his clock. It was three a.m.

"What is it, Angus?" What do you hear?" Angus continued his long deep rumbling. Just then Mark heard it. Footsteps on the roof, directly overhead.

"Not again," he said wearily. "Rocky Raccoon up to his old tricks. Let's go, boy."

Groping around in the dark, he searched the floor for his slippers. Ignoring his robe, he hurried out to the living room in his pajamas, Angus close on his heels. He threw open the door and Angus dashed ahead, racing off into the darkness---barking and charging after some unseen prey.

Mark rushed through the door, yelling for Angus to stop. Suddenly something brushed past his face, soft and sticky. He stumbled back, raising his hands to shield his face. Mark looked out into the blackness but could see nothing. He reached back and turned on the living room chandelier.

Suspended over the front door, hanging upside-down from the eaves, were the lifeless bodies of two white doves. Their heads had been severed. Mark looked down at his hands, which were covered with congealing blood. Blood was all over the front of his pajamas as well.

Bile burned his throat as he leaned against the door jamb, fighting back a wave of nausea.

Chapter 10

Mark could hear Angus barking up in the hills behind the monastery. Looking back at the birds as they swung back and forth in the doorway, he was again repulsed. His eyes were drawn down to his bloodied hands and his stomach turned.

He pulled the mutilated birds down and tossed them into a nearby waste can. His knees were weak and he couldn't stop shaking.

Mark quickly surveyed the courtyard to be sure he was alone. He hurried back into the house and quickly bolted the door. Leaning against the wood panel, he swallowed hard, trying to hold back the vomit that threatened to erupt.

Realizing that Angus was still outside, it took a concentrated effort to re-open the door. Visions of mutilated dogs and cats flooded his mind. He threw back the dead bolt and opened the door as he called out to his dog. There was no answering bark, but he thought he heard the rustling of leaves on the other side of the garden wall.

"Angus, come here, right now!" he ordered as he walked to the gate. For once Angus ignored his command. Sprinting across the field toward the highway were two silhouettes. Tripping and flailing about, it looked as though something was tangled around their ankles. A darker shadow was bouncing above the tall grass nipping at calves and heels. It was Angus in hot pursuit.

"Here, boy," he yelled. "Come, Angus." But the dog was relentless in his pursuit of the night stalkers. Realizing that Angus would not come back until he was ready, Mark said a quick prayer to St. Francis and returned to the house.

Throwing the dead bold, he quickly looked around to check for intruders. Confident that he was alone in the house, Mark headed for the bathroom. He threw his bloodied pajamas into the sink and stepped into the shower. He let the hot, steaming water pour over him as he watched the blood run down his body. It circled around his feet in a pale pink stain before disappearing into the swirling vortex around the drain.

Anxiety slowly turned into anger. The security of his world had been breached. He was being stalked. The water began to run cool and he wondered how long he had been standing in the shower.

Knowing there could be no more sleep tonight, Mark put on a pot of coffee, poured himself a brandy and dumped his pajamas and slippers into the washing machine. Beginning to truly worry about Angus now, Mark unlocked the door and stepped outside, avoiding the congealed blood that had pooled around the doorstep.

"Angus! Angus!" he shouted. Getting no response, he again asked St. Francis to protect his courageous little friend. Walking out to the carport, he hooked up a hose to the water spigot and washed down the doorstep, sending slippery red rivulets into the crevices of the flagstone courtyard.

Taking a broom, he scrubbed away the last vestiges of the night's mischief.

Rewinding the hose, Mark looked up to the monastery and noticed a golden strip of light edging the hills. As the priest stood there with the broom in his hand, he offered up a silent prayer of thanksgiving, grateful to see this night come to an end. The band of gold became wider and wider as he watched the hills come alive with the colors of the morning. He watched birds as they flew from tree to tree and a deer as it bounded out of the woods and into the field, her fawn close behind. The world was waking up and with the daylight came a renewed sense of control. Mark resolved that he would get to the bottom of this.

The priest turned back into the house and poured himself a strong cup of coffee. After a couple of mugs, Mark felt calm enough to call Tim. Unfortunately, it was not yet seven and Tim was not in his office so Mark left a message for his friend to call him. Grabbing a sweater, he headed over to the chapel to prepare for morning Mass.

It was with a great sense of relief that Mark read a note waiting for him on the counter in the sacristy. Mother Benedicta wanted him to know that Angus was found scratching at the convent gate during the early hours of the morning, and was now esconced in the convent garden.

"Would Father please be good enough to retrieve his errant companion right after Mass?" the letter read. "His charm was proving to be an irresistable distraction to the novices."

Mark smiled as he put the letter down. "Thanks, St. Francis, you came through again," he said.

Reunited, priest and dog returned to the white-washed cottage. In the clear morning sunshine, it was almost impossible to believe the events of last night had really happened. The garden was lovely in the early morning. Bright fuchsia bougainvillea crawled over the walls and yellow roses next to lavender hibiscus and golden cymbidiums were sending out their fragrant call to honey bees and humming birds.

Standing there drinking in such beauty, Mark could almost believe last night was just a nightmare, a dark and ugly dream, were it not for the broken glass around the outdoor lights. Walking past the garbage can, he could see the bloody doves lying on the bottom.

The shrill ringing of the telephone pulled Mark back to the present and he hurried in to answer it.

"Good morning. Father Ross here."

"Hello, Father. It's me, Shelby."

"How are you this morning?" he asked.

"I'm much better, but the doctor wants me to stay in the hospital for a few days. For observation, he said, but…"

"That's a good idea, Shelby." Mark cut her off. "I think you should stay there."

"But, Father," the girl said, "I'm frightened for you. I know they saw me talking to you and I can't stop thinking about Miss Wayland."

"Shelby, you are not to blame for what happened to Miss Wayland. It was an accident, a tragic accident. And I can take care of myself."

"I know, Father, but I can't stop thinking about her. And now they know about you. I am afraid to tell my parents, I am afraid of what might happen to them."

"Shelby, I want you to promise me that you will try to stay calm, stay where you are and let me help you."

"Okay," she reluctantly agreed, "but please be very careful. Promise?"

"I promise. Good-bye." Mark replaced the phone in its cradle and stood there remembering the previous night. Well, at least nothing will happen in broad daylight, he thought. Perhaps a short run would clear his mind. The sleepless night had left him feeling dazed. Before he could leave the house, the phone rang again.

"Hello."

"Padre, Tim here. Glad I caught you. I just heard from the mechanic that looked at Shelby's car. He swears that there is nothing wrong with those brakes."

"Then what do you make of the accident, Tim?"

"Well, the only thing I can think is that either she mistook the brake pedal for the accelerator or that she might very well have been the victim of some mumbo-jumbo."

"Tim, I think Shelby is right about the kids getting involved in some form of witchcraft or Satanic rituals."

"What's happened?"

"Yesterday I visited Marissa Bentley's bookstore. It's filled with New Age books, witchcraft, crystals, tarot cards---the works. And while I was there, a teenager came in that fit the description that Shelby gave me of one of the members of the coven."

"Did you get a chance to talk to the owner?"

"Oh, yes. We had quite a lively conversation. I also got a good look at that medallion she wears around her neck. It's a copy of an ancient amulet worn by a group that called themselves The Order of the Knights Templar." Mark continued.

"And then last night I had some unwelcome visitors. At first I thought it was just some kids getting into some harmless Halloween mischief, but now I think someone is trying to scare me off. In the middle of the night, someone left two decapitated white doves on my door."

"Sounds to me like you're making someone uncomfortable. You could be in real trouble down here, Padre."

"I know. But don't worry, I intend to watch my back from now on."

"Better yet, why not let me watch it for you? I was going to call you this morning even if you hadn't called. Mary wanted me to come down there to keep you company for a few days. She's worried about you. And I cleared it with my Chief. So if no one is using the guest room, I'd like to move in."

"That's great, Tim. I could use your help. I'm the first to admit it when I am in over my head. These jokers play a little too rough."

"Swell. I'm just about to leave. I should be there before noon."

"Angus and I were about to head out for a run. We'll be back in plenty of time to fix lunch."

"Stay in busy areas, don't go off by yourself."

"Don't worry. I'm just going to run down the highway to Point Lobos and back."

"Okay, Father, see you soon."

"Bye, Tim. And thanks."

Ten minutes later, Mark and Angus were jogging south on Highway One towards Point Lobos. In the distance, a lone pine stood vigil on the edge of the cliff. That pine had been made famous by so many painters and photographers, that it had become practically an icon for the Monterey peninsula.

Mark had seen it in pictures a hundred times or more long before his first visit to Carmel. He always used it as a marker on his runs. It was just about two miles from the monastery and a comfortable distance for a run. There was an old whaler's cove just below the point that made a nice spot to rest and meditate.

Today, though, Mark didn't make his usual stop. He turned at the Point and began the trek home. It was a perfect October day, cool and sunny.

His attention was suddenly drawn to a distant speck cresting the hill on the highway just ahead. A red car was heading toward him at what seemed a great speed. It was coming straight for him.

He quickly assessed his options and there weren't many. He could try to cross the road and head up the hillside, but he would most probably be hit by a car in the other lane---and there was almost no shoulder on the ocean side of the road.

Pure instinct for survival took over and Mark dove out of the way of the oncoming car. He landed on the soft shoulder of the road, too close to the edge. The cliff was weak and the ground crumbled away under him, sending an avalanche of rocks and dirt to the beach below.

Clawing at the decorative vines of iceplant lining the highway, he tried to regain his hold, but it was impossible and he started to slide backwards over the edge. He saw the red car rocketing past him as he fell into empty space.

Rolling and sliding down the steep embankment, Mark felt a sharp pain in his shoulder. His head repeatedly banged against rocks and outcroppings. His hands reached out, trying to grasp at bushes or small shrubs---anything to stop his furious rolling. But he continued to barrel down the hillside towards the water.

Head over heels he plummeted down, finally coming to rest with a sickening thud against a sand dune nearly two hundred feet below the busy highway. Thick clouds of sand and dust rolled over him, clogging his nostrils and burning his throat. He tried to sit up to check for broken bones, but he couldn't move.

Voices from above, mixed with Angus's barking, came to him from what seemed a great distance and he tried to open his eyes. They burned from the sand that had lodged under his eyelids.

Though his vision was blurred, he could see men crawling down the cliffs to him. Angus led the rescue party is a crazy rush to reach his master first.

"Don't move, Mister. I called 911 on my car phone as soon as I saw you go off the side of the road. Help should be here any minute."

Mark tried to speak, but only a low croak escaped his throat. His head felt like a tree had fallen on it and he was sure most of his skin had been scraped off. Angus's large brown eyes looked into his face---it was the last thing Mark saw as he lost consciousness.

Chapter 11

Mark squinted, turning away from the blinding light that greeted his return to consciousness. The painful glare seemed to explode around him, rousing him from the comfortable twilight of semi-consciousness. Trying to shield his eyes, he was suddenly aware of a hand gripping his wrist.

Forcing his eyes open, they gradually came into focus around the person standing at his bedside. The young nurse taking his pulse smiled down at him.

"Well, welcome back."

"Where am I?" asked the priest.

"Peninsula Community Hospital. You had an accident and the police brought you here to the emergency room."

She was interrupted by an angry voice. "Accident my foot! It was a hit and run. Your guardian angel must be working overtime, Padre." Looming over the shoulder of the diminutive nurse, the six-foot form of Lt. Tim Bryant slowly came into view. "You had me worried for a few minutes there. How are you feeling?"

"Sore. A little dizzy. How should I feel?" Mark asked, looking at the nurse.

"You have a concussion and you're pretty banged up and bruised, but it doesn't look like any bones are broken."

Mark tried to sit up on the gurney but the young nurse pushed him back down.

"None of that now, not until the doctor checks you out."

"Do you remember anything, Mark?" Tim asked, stepping closer to the gurney.

His head was clearing quickly now. "Angus and I were out for a run and...Angus! Where's my dog, Tim?" "Don't worry about him. He's faster on four legs than you are on two. He's fine," Tim reassured him.

Relieved, Mark's thoughts went back to the last thing he remembered before going over the embankment. "There was a car, red I think...older model. I didn't get a good look at the driver. It all happened so fast."

"Well, the police have a couple of witnesses, but they're not much help to us. Both were several hundred feet behind you, and on the other side of the road. One is sure that the car was brown and the other that it was red. One swears it was a Mercury, the other that it was a Mustang. But both are agreed on one thing---whoever it was seemed to swerve into you deliberately. I've already talked to the Carmel Police. There is an officer down the hall waiting to see if you can give a statement."

A young man in blue jeans and a white lab coat approached the gurney. "Hi, I'm Doctor Bonner. How are you feeling?" Mark explained that aside from a headache and some dizziness, he was feeling fine. The intern glanced at the chart attached to the gurney, then went through the customary rituals, taking Mark's pulse again and pressing a cold stethoscope against his chest.

"I'd like to keep you overnight just to be on the safe side. With a concussion, even a minor one like yours, it's always better to err on the side of caution."

Mark's protests, coupled with the policeman's declared intention of staying with him overnight, was enough to cause the young doctor to relent and he agreed to discharge him with a list of instructions.

After giving his statement to the Carmel policeman, Mark said, "Tim, since we're here, I think we'd better make a visit upstairs to see Shelby. Someone has obviously decided to play rough. It's hard to say now what he might do next."

They found Shelby dressed and sitting in a chair by the window. Anne Townsend was busy hovering over an open suitcase on the bed packing up her daughter's belongings. The young girl's face lit up as soon as she saw the priest but her expression instantly turned anxious when she noticed the condition he was in.

"Father Ross, what happened to you?" she asked, unable to conceal her alarm. Her Mother spun around.

Michael Townsend stepped forward from his place in the corner. He put his arm around the priest's shoulder and guided him to a chair. Shaking Tim's hand he said, "Mr. Bryant, good to see you again. But may I ask what is going on?"

Both Tim and Mark looked at Shelby. "Shelby, I think it is time to tell your parents," Tim said.

She looked from priest to policeman and back again. "Yes, I know, Lt. Bryant."

"Lt. Bryant? I repeat, just what is going on?" a very disturbed father asked.

"Daddy, Mom, it all started last spring. Some of the kids started going to the occult bookstore in town and then someone got the idea to try a little 'white witchcraft'."

"Witchcraft? What are you saying?" Anne interrupted.

"Well, we thought it was harmless at first. But I know better now. There is no 'white witchcraft'. It's all black and evil." The girl began to cry.

"It's all right, Shelby, take your time," Tim said softly, encouraging her while he handed her a tiny tissue from the miniature box of hospital tissues.

Shelby smiled up at him gratefully. "At first it was fun. You know, kind of mysterious and scary. But then things began to get out of hand. One night, Stacy showed up with black robes that had hoods. One for each of us. And then things began to happen, like Jeff getting his uncle's car, and our team winning the championship. And then you and Daddy getting back together again."

"I don't understand. What did our separation have to do with any of this?" Michael seemed confused.

"That was what I asked for, Daddy. That you and Mom should get back together and we would be a family again."

"Oh, darling, I'm so sorry. I didn't realize how deeply we had hurt you." Now Anne, too, began to weep.

"Anne, let the girl talk." Michael broke in, somewhat impatiently.

Mark poured a glass of water for the distraught girl. She took it and continued her story. "Then everyone started to get really weird. They began to call themselves the Crystal Coven. And they started killing small animals for sacrifice. I told them I was not going to be part of the group anymore. I was too scared and really sick about the animals. But they said 'once a member, always a member'. They said I could not quit, that I was in forever."

"Shelby, why didn't you come to us?" her father asked.

"I don't know. I guess I was afraid that you'd be disappointed in me."

"We would never be disappointed in you, darling. Your father and I are very proud of you. We love you very much," Anne affirmed. Michael nodded in agreement.

"I did try to get some advice. I went to my counselor, Miss Wayland."

"Oh, my God!" Anne recognized the name. "She's the young woman who drowned last week."

"Yes. And it was all my fault." A flood of tears broke loose and Shelby fell into her mother's arms.

"There is no proof yet that the kids had anything to do with her death. And even if there was, you're not responsible for what they might have done," Tim said. "Shelby, you've got to stop blaming yourself. It was not your fault." He tried to relieve her of some of her guilt feelings, knowing what would happen if she continued to dwell on these thoughts.

"I can't help it, Lt. Bryant. What about my car? And what happened to Father Ross?" she argued.

"Well, that's why we came to see you," Tim explained. "Last night someone paid a late night visit to Father Ross and left him a couple of headless birds. And then this afternoon, someone ran him off the road while he was running."

Anne Townsend's face went from nervous apprehension to near panic. She held her daughter tightly in her arms as if to shield her from danger with her own body.

"Dear God, what are we going to do? I can't believe this is happening. When is it going to stop?"

Michael went to her side and wrapped his arms around his family.

"I don't want to scare you, but I do think we have real cause for concern here," Tim went on. "It's no longer a simple case of intimidation. We've gone from mutilated animals and scare tactics to what may be attempted murder. And there is still Janet Wayland's death to consider."

"Can't you arrest someone? At least bring Jeff and Stacy in for questioning?" asked Shelby's father.

"I wish it were that simple," answered Tim. "But I'm a member of the San Francisco Police Department, not the Carmel Police. I am not in my jurisdiction here and I'm afraid that the policemen that I have spoken with are not very interested in my theories. In my experience, these kinds of cases are very difficult to prosecute. A few years ago we had a case involving the cult abuse of some children in a day-care center at Presidio Army Base in San Francisco."

He continued, "A high ranking army officer who also moonlighted as high priest of a New Age cult was implicated. Despite the testimony of many of the children, the D.A.'s office ended up dropping the case and the army officer was quietly transferred and promoted. He was an adult, his involvement in the occult was undisputed, we had the testimony of the children and we still lost."

Tim added, "Here we're talking about kids, teenagers. And as far as witnesses go, at least in Father Mark's case, all we have is the conflicting testimony of two drivers who can't even agree on the color or make of the car that went after him. Do you see what I'm getting at? Even if we could arrest one or another of the kids on suspicion, I don't think we could hold them for long. And that still leaves the others free to do God knows what."

"Are you telling me that we're helpless? That there's nothing we can do but sit here and be victims?" Mike asked.

"No, Mr. Townsend, there's always something that can be done," Mark said. "But it depends on just how far you are willing to go for your family. What sacrifices you are willing to make."

Michael stood still, turning things over in his mind. "Father, are you suggesting we just up and leave town?"

"Yes, that's exactly what I mean," the priest answered.

"Our home? Our work? Shelby's school?" Anne asked, stunned. "All we've worked so hard for...for so long?"

"We can't do that, Father," Mike answered.

"I don't think you really know what danger you're in," said the priest. "Shelby's here now because of their anger. Lord knows what will happen next."

"Nothing," Mike responded. "Nothing is going to happen to my little girl. I won't let them near her."

"How can you watch her twenty-four hours a day? There is only one of you and thirteen of them." Mark tried to reason with him.

"I'm here too, you know," Anne stepped in. "She's my daughter too."

"Yes," Tim said, "but you aren't dealing with normal kid pranks."

"With all due respect, Lieutenant," Mike answered, "I think we can take care of ourselves. After all, they're still just kids."

"No they are not," Mark warned. "These are dangerous kids being manipulated by a devious grown up."

"But Father," Anne said, "we can't just walk away from our careers, our home, our friends."

"She's right. I won't let them drive us out," Mike declared.

"What can I say that will make you both see how dangerous it is to stay here?" Tim sighed. "These people are not playing games. And the way they see it, Shelby has betrayed them."

"Thank you both for your concern," Mike said. "But I think you are overreacting to this whole thing. We'll take precautions with Shelby's friends."

"Friends! Haven't you been listening?" Tim sounded exasperated.

"My husband is right," Anne agreed. "One of us will be with her at all times."

A feeling of futility filled the two friends as they took their leave.

"What do you make of that, Padre?" asked Tim as they waited for an elevator.

"I don't know what else we could have said, Tim. But we have to look at this from their point of view. After all, this is the nineties. Witches and devils are a thing of the past. Most people today don't want to think they are real. They belong in the Dark Ages with dragons and sorcerers."

Standing in the hospital parking lot, both men felt a common sense of depression, as though they were waiting for the other shoe to fall.

Trying to break the sense of gloom, Tim asked, "How about some dinner?"

"Where would you suggest?"

"How about the Pine Inn?" he asked.

"Are you buying?"

"Only because I've tasted your cooking," Tim said with a laugh.

"Better head for home to change clothes and shower first," Mark said. "I don't think we would pass the Pine Inn's dress code with torn running shorts and a bloody T-shirt."

As they drove down the hospital driveway, the devastating effects of the fire could be seen. What should have been a lush green blanket of pine forest had been reduced to charred skeletons of trees and blackened earth. It was apparent that the holocaust had been halted only yards from the hospital grounds.

Only the two-lane road stood between the awful scene of destruction and the verdant lawns of the hospital. Just as they reached the bottom of the drive and prepared to turn out on to the road, a glint of metal reflecting in the sunshine caught Mark's eye.

"Stop the car, Tim."

Mark got out and walked over to the shining object suspended in the tree. The heat from the fire across the road had been so intense that the side of the tree facing the road was scorched while the hospital side was still green and alive. Hanging in the midst of the burnt bark and singed pine needles was a slightly warped holy medal of St. Michael the Archangel.

****

"You fool! You young idiot!" Jeff Archer stood trembling before the verbal blast being directed against him by his mentor.

"Since when have you become smart enough to start thinking on your own? Do you really think you are powerful enough to challenge my authority? Do you see yourself as my successor already?"

"But that's not what I was trying to do," pleaded the teenager, clenching his fists to keep his hands from shaking. "I just wanted to scare him. I didn't even hit him. I just thought..."

"That's just the trouble. You thought! And your stupid blunder may have cost us everything. Now the police are involved. There are witnesses."

The lanky adolescent stood staring at his shoes, unable any longer to meet the malevolent glare of his enraged teacher. In a final flash of courage, he said. "I knew Shelby had seen him and talked to him. I wanted to scare him, make him back off. I was only trying to protect us."

"Protect us! By running him down in broad daylight with witnesses everywhere? What you did put us all in jeopardy. Right now your only duty is to obey."

"But what about Wayland? What if she told him about Wayland?" Jeff's voice sounded whiny and high-pitched and he hated himself for his weakness.

"Wayland! It was over and done with. A stupid woman falls into the ocean and drowns. Suicide or accident, it doesn't matter. Case closed! Now, thanks to your stupidity, the police may start looking deeper. Besides, there are other ways of handling Father Mark Ross."

"All right, all right, I'm sorry." Jeff's face was contorted in a petulant scowl. As soon as he'd uttered the words he knew he'd made a mistake. Self-justification was one thing, but remorse, penitence was not tolerated in his new creed.

"Sorry!" Her voice cracked with rage.

A clammy sweat broke over him. He held his breath. He listened, bracing himself for the torrent of abuse that he knew must follow. But what chilled him more than anything was the long, unbearable silence.

He raised his eyes to meet her awful gaze and felt the gorge rise to his throat as he beheld the contempt in her eyes. He wasn't powerful. He was an insect sent back down to the foot of the class. When she spoke, her voice was clipped and cruel.

"You have one chance to redeem yourself. And I mean one chance. Do you understand?"

Jeff nodded, brightening at the possibility of a reprieve.

"We need a replacement to complete the circle. You are going to supply that replacement. Is that clear? And don't make the mistake you made with Shelby."

Recognizing a way out of his predicament, the teen grasped at his commission like a drowning man reaching for a life preserver.

"I think I may have someone who I can recruit. His name is Bob Everett. He has some weaknesses that I think I can work to our advantage."

"What is he like? Does his family go to Church? Is he baptized into that faith our Master finds so offensive?" She drilled her pupil.

"He's a loner. He isn't into sports and doesn't belong to any clubs. I don't think he has any brothers or sisters. His folks are divorced and his father lives in Arizona or someplace like that. I'm sure he doesn't go to church because he is always hanging around the beach on weekends."

"What weaknesses does he have that might be exploited?"

"I know he is a stoner and he drinks a lot too."

"Promising, but I'll want to see some results."

"I could use the Ouija Board again. It's worked with others. I'll ask him to join us at the house. Maybe this weekend. If he goes along with the Board, then I'll invite him in on a little experiment, maybe a spell."

"Can you do this on your own or will you need my help?"

"I can do it. Let me prove it to you." The eager young boy tried to regain some semblance of pride.

"You will need some candles."

"Yes, I remember. Green candles for money, red candles for love and black candles to reap revenge against an enemy."

"Good. At least you haven't forgotten that. Do you remember how to make a wax doll and what to do with it? Tonight may be a good time for a refresher course."

"What do we do about Shelby? She isn't going to stay quiet."

"Oh, I think we'll have to arrange something special for Miss Townsend. Maybe something that will kill two birds with one stone, shall we say?"

****

Rolling gently down from the highway through quaint shops and fashionable boutiques, Ocean Avenue---Carmel's main street---terminated in a beautiful white sand beach at the foot of the Village. Always a favorite gathering place for both natives and tourists, especially at sunset, the beach provided front row seats to nature's nightly spectacle. When the sky was aflame with luminous shades of purple, pink and gold, and the Pacific breezes heavy with the scent of some faraway exotic shore, it was easy to appreciate the local legend that Robert Louis Stevenson had received his inspiration for the novel "Treasure Island" here.

For a while, Stevenson had taken up residence at the Pine Inn on Ocean Avenue. Every time Mark walked into the lobby with it's red flocked wall paper, polished brass spitoons and plush Victorian settees, he thought of Stevenson. "Treasure Island" had been one of his favorite books as a child, and it always pleased him to think that he and Stevenson shared a love of these same golden sunsets.

Just beyond the lobby lay the dining room. Mark and Tim were conducted to their table by an impeccably dressed waiter with an affected air and a very expensive haircut. As they followed the young man across the dimly lit room, Tim surveyed the red flocked wallpaper and massive crystal chandeliers.

"I always feel like I've wandered into a Victorian bordello by mistake," Tim whispered. Mark hushed his friend with a roll of his eyes.

They settled themselves into surprisingly uncomfortable chairs and were handed menus along with a review of the evening's specials. Mark ordered an old fashioned and Tim a scotch and soda. By the time they were finished with their second round of drinks, their chairs no longer felt quite so uncomfortable. The two friends were feeling warm and relaxed as they talked about family and old times.

Spearing the cherry at the bottom of his glass with a swizzle stick, Mark changed the topic. "You know, sitting here like this, it's hard to remember that all this Satanic stuff is real. And yet we've experienced it. You read about it in police files. I read about it in seminary classes, but it's all so bizarre and out of the realm of our ordinary experience that it seems unreal. Even when you've been through it."

"Why do you think these cases are so hard to prosecute?" the veteran cop responded.

Suddenly Mark caught his breath. He stared past his friend, to the other side of the room. "Just when you think it might all have been an overactive imagination, up pops the devil." Mark said, nodding toward the doorway.

Tim turned to see a very attractive, dark-haired woman with another not-so-attractive younger woman waiting by the door to be seated.

"Marissa Bentley and one of her proteges," Mark explained. Let's have a word with the Voodoo Queen of Carmel." The priest was on his feet in an instant. Tim reached out and grabbed his friend's wrist.

"Mark, wait. Remember, we don't yet have any solid proof. Any confrontation now could backfire on us. She could come back at you with harassment and defamation charges. I've seen it happen before."

"Just a word, that's all I want with her. Just a friendly chat. Don't worry, I'll be good," said Mark through clenched teeth. Pulling free of his friend's grasp, the priest made his way across the crowded room with a speed that caught Marissa by surprise. The priest was suddenly in her face before she had time to make a strategic withdrawal.

"Well, if it isn't the wicked witch of the West Coast. And who's this? Dorothy?" Mark said in a tone that turned the heads of the diners nearby.

"What a surprise," retorted Marissa, not bothering to conceal her contempt. "You look a little worse for wear. Perhaps Carmel isn't such a healthy climate after all."

"The gloves are off, Marissa. Let's not pretend we both don't know what's really going on here. Your nasty little secret's out. People are on to you now and it's only a matter of time before someone cracks and comes clean. It'll be all over for you then."

"You know, holy man, I've grown tired of our little dialogues. I suggest you go back to your monastery if you know what's good for you. Better yet, go back to your frightened flock in San Francisco. Perhaps you can scare them with your fairy stories, but you don't intimidate me."

Just then Tim caught up with his friend. Smiling, the priest said, "Marissa, allow me to introduce my friend, Lt. Tim Bryant of the San Francisco Police Department. He is one of my frightened flock."

A look of pure hatred transformed Marissa Bentley's beautiful features into a contorted mask. Eyes blazing, she turned and strode toward the door, pulling the young woman in black beside her.

Mark called after her. "Looking into my crystal ball, I see a career change looming in your near future, Marissa. Hope you enjoy making license plates as much as you do casting spells!"

"I have no idea what you are talking about," she answered as she walked through the door.

An anxious maitre'd stood nearby wringing his hands, the perfect picture of sheer mortification.

"Gentlemen, please," he hissed in a voice that sounded like steam escaping from a radiator.

"If that's what you call being good, Padre, I'd hate to see what you mean by bad," said the policeman with a low whistle.

"Sorry," said Mark, "but her kind flourishes in the darkness. I just wanted her to know there will be no more games, no more clever banter. Let her go on the defensive for a change."

The confrontation with Marissa Bentley actually seemed to sharpen Mark's appetite and lift his spirits. After dinner, they decided to walk around the corner to the Hog's Breath Inn for a nightcap. The beauty of the sunset had long since faded into blackness and the fog had moved in like a dark tide, bringing a chill into the night air.

Part of the charm of the Hog's Breath lay in the many outdoor fireplaces and cozy conversation pits nestled in its sunken patio. But not even the warmth of the mesquite fire glowing in the chimney could dispel the clammy coldness of the night.

The chill of the night air prodded them to quickly finish their drinks and retrace their steps to where they had parked the car behind the Pine Inn.

It was past eleven when their headlamps caught the Moorish tower and red tile roof of the chapel as they drove up the steep drive to the monastery.

On the cottage door they found a note from Mother Benedicta:

Dear Father Ross,

We called the hospital and they informed us that you had been discharged. Praise be God! We have Angus, so don't worry. You can pick him up in the morning after Mass.

My Glory, what a day this has been for you. I know that the day after tomorrow is All Saints' Day, but we don't want you joining the Heavenly Multitude just yet.

Do be careful. If you are not up to saying Mass, phone us in the morning.

In Jesus, Mother B.

Mark smiled and handed the note to Tim. "Ditto," said the cop, scanning the note.

Mark clapped his hand on his friend's shoulder. "Tim, I want to thank you for everything. Once again, you've been a great friend."

"Sleep well, Padre," Tim said and headed down the hall to his room.

After Tim had closed the bedroom door behind him, Mark proceeded to lock up the house and turn out the lights. When all was secure, he changed into his pajamas and slipped gratefully into the bed between clean white sheets. Every muscle in his body ached. Reaching for the lamp on the bed table, he suddenly remembered that in the chaos of the day, he hadn't finished his prayers. He was certain he had left his breviary on the bench in the garden.

Padding barefoot across the cool clay tiles, he stepped out onto the patio into the damp night. The pounding of the surf always seemed louder at night, but now it was overwhelming, sending rhythmic shock waves against the house.

He used to love the sound of the ocean at night. It had always been soothing to him, like being rocked to sleep. But now it seemed foreboding, part of an atmosphere that was charged with some unseen and threatening presence.

Like the crashing surf from the beach below, the fear started to well up within him and wash over him in waves. All at once he felt like a six-year-old child again, alone and afraid of the dark.

A vague and faceless fear crystallized in his mind, assuming the grotesque image of a headless dove twisting slowly in the breeze. He wondered if he could ever step into the darkness again without fearing the sickening caress of that warm, soft wetness.

Mark fought an overpowering urge to look back over his shoulder. Part of him wanted to run back to the warm comforting embrace of the well-lit cottage. Forcing himself forward into the shadows, he came to the garden bench. In the light flooding into the garden from the open door, he could clearly see that the prayer book was not there.

He looked on the small table and under the chair--- no breviary anywhere. A shiver passed through his body as he stepped over the threshold into the warm golden glow of the living room. Like a wet spaniel, he shook off the chill and continued his search, looking in all the usual places. Unable to retrieve his book, Mark decided to continue the search in the morning.

Returning to his room, Mark was unable to shake off the damp chill that still clung to him. Deciding to exchange his pajama shirt for something warmer, he reached for a sweatshirt hanging on a hook near the closet.

Pulling the pajama shirt over his head, he suddenly caught sight of himself in the mirror on the closet door. Looking over his shoulder, he was startled to see horizontal lines across the width of his back---deep red lines that had the appearance of whip marks.

As he watched, the crimson stripes grew more and more pronounced until his back was crisscrossed in angry red welts. In the distance, Mark could hear the clock tower in the village tolling the hour.

****

In a hidden room across town, the final stroke of midnight could still be heard reverberating through empty streets as the pages of Father Mark Ross's breviary were slowly being torn from their binding and dropped one by one into a fire burning in an antique brazier. In the glow of black candles, another set of hands slowly coiled a leather thong around a curious little wax doll dressed in a black robe and white collar.

Chapter 12

Wednesday morning found Mark and Tim walking together in silence to the chapel for Mass, deep in their own thoughts.

They stopped under an apricot tree to look out over the beautiful blue waters of the Pacific. Just below them, they could see Monastery Beach with its white sands and teal blue water. There were several large outcroppings of rocks along the water's edge that served as breakfast tables for sea gulls and terns. Later on in the day, the same boulders might very well be used by a family to spread their picnic lunch on.

"Now I ask you, Padre, how could such a beautiful place be such a den of evil?"

"That's a good question. Just how does evil take hold in a place like this? I wish I knew. Perhaps it's like Edmund Burke said: 'All it takes for evil to flourish is for good people to do nothing.'"

"I think he was right. Most people don't want to see what's happening. It's easier to keep their heads buried in the sand. They don't want to disturb their tidy little lives, so they just ignore the signs and keep on pretending everything is status quo." They both noticed that there were several cars in the parking lot and several more climbing the drive.

"Time to get inside," Mark said. "See you after Mass."

"Okay, Father. By the way, what are you going to say about that shiner and those cuts and scrapes? You look like you've been run over by a truck."

"Not a thing, Tim. Maybe no one will notice." Mark laughed as he turned away to enter the sacristy door.

Tim stood watching his friend walk away. When Mark was safely inside, he went around to the front of the chapel and entered through the main entrance with the other daily communicants. He didn't want to let on to Mark just how worried he was, but he had been dealing with these bastards for a long time now and he had a healthy respect for the devils.

As he knelt before Mass, Tim invoked his favorite saint, St. Michael the Archangel. He was not only the patron saint of policemen, he was the saint to be sought out for protection from the devil.

Tim had little doubt that that was indeed who they were dealing with. If he had any doubts before, last night's episode had dispelled them. This was not just a bunch of restless, bored kids fooling around. The stench of fire and brimstone permeated this whole affair.

Tim had worked the 'devil squad' for several years. Not too many people were aware that all major police departments around the country had a particular squad that dealt with witchcraft, Satanism and children's disappearances. Few also knew that many of the missing children were taken for human sacrifice.

As Mass began, Tim looked around the chapel. Would these good, God-fearing folks believe that here in this sleepy little village, they sheltered such evil? He doubted it. Most good people believed that witches and Satanists died out in the Middle Ages, if indeed they had ever existed. But in fact, they had only been driven underground, to arise stronger and more and more defiant.

Mark stepped out of the sacristy and entered the sanctuary ready to begin Mass, but as he turned to the people, he heard an audible gasp from the pews. He knew he must say something to the congregation before the opening prayer or very few of them would be able to concentrate on the Mass.

"Before we begin, let us offer a prayer for all those who will be on the highways this day. As you can see, I was another victim of Highway One yesterday. Nothing serious, just few scrapes and bruises, folks. Believe me, it looks much worse than it really is."

He smiled out at the many concerned faces and hoped that his explanation would be accepted.

"Now let us pray."

With Mass completed, Mark took a few minutes to meet with Mother Benedicta. Her concern was genuine when she saw Mark wince as he took his seat on his side of the grille.

"Good morning, Father. I'm sorry to say this, but you resemble something the cat dragged in and then threw back out." Her sense of humor didn't hide her anxiety.

"Good morning, Mother," he answered.

"You know, Father, the sisters are praying for you. We are all very worried. Satan is a powerful enemy and he won't give up easily. There are a great many souls at stake here, and your life might very well be in jeopardy. What happened to you yesterday was a very clear warning. You must be very careful not to let your guard down."

"Believe me, Mother, I intend to watch my back at all times. I am very grateful for your prayers. By all accounts I should have been dead, or at least seriously injured yesterday."

"And what is happening with the girl?" the old nun asked.

"She left the hospital yesterday afternoon, Mother. Tim and I helped Shelby to talk with her parents. I think they're aware of the danger but are not sure what course of action to take. Please continue to pray for her."

"Have no fear of that---you are all in our prayers. By the way, are you wearing your St. Michael medal?"

"Yes, Mother, and I almost forgot to tell you that I found one of your medals hanging in a tree across from the hospital. The fire had stopped exactly where the medals were hung in the trees along the drive."

"You act somewhat surprised, Father. Oh ye of little faith," she said in feigned reproof.

"Don't fool yourself, Mother---I never let a day go by that I don't ask St. Michael for his help. And I know that Tim is also very devoted to St. Michael."

"I know that you have God on your side, but I am very happy that you also have Lt. Tim Bryant. He is a good man."

Mother Benedicta smiled as she stood to leave. "Please be assured of our continued prayers, and keep me informed of your progress."

"I will. Thank you." Mark stood as the grille closed behind the retreating nun.

He hurried back to the priest's house as fast as his sore muscles would permit. He was welcomed by the aroma of freshly-brewed coffee.

"Come on in, Padre. Have a seat," Tim called out. "A bit of breakfast should be in order and then I think we'll try to find the abandoned house Shelby talked about."

"Good thinking, Tim," the grateful priest said. "I'd like to know once and for all what we are dealing with."

"I know exactly what we are dealing with. I just want some idea of how deep these kids are in. Boy, this is great bread."

Mark smiled at his friend as he watched Tim pile butter and home-made jam on a healthy slice of whole wheat.

"Sister Paula will be pleased to hear how much you like her bread. It's one of my favorite bonuses when I visit the sisters."

"Just exactly where did Shelby say the kids were meeting?" Tim asked, as he prepared another slice of bread.

"An abandoned house in the Highlands. I remember, because I was surprised that there was an abandoned building there. It's a beautiful community and very much in demand. Nothing stays on the market long in that neighborhood."

"Where are the Highlands?" Tim asked.

"Just south of here. The homes are terraced along the side of the Santa Lucia Mountain Range in the hills above the Highlands Inn."

"Did she mention anything that would help us identify it?"

"Just that it was abandoned, on a hillside, very isolated and difficult to see from the road. Except for being abandoned, it might be any house in the Highlands," Mark added.

"Think about what else she might have said," Tim coaxed.

"Wait a minute. She said there were several signs posted about the property---No Hunting, No Trespassing, that kind of stuff."

"Well, what do you say we do a little hunting and trespassing? Just to see if we can find it." Tim placed his dishes in the dishwasher.

Mark said, "I can see this is going to be one of those occasions when I am glad you wear a badge for a living."

"Maybe for this excursion you might want to change out of your uniform and into a pair of jeans. But take your holy water, just in case."

Mark realized that Tim was only half joking.

The men headed south and turned east at the Highlands Inn. A low whistle escaped Tim's lips as he looked up into the hills at the terraces. Tall stands of pine trees and deep ravines provided some really exceptional homesites.

"I'm impressed," he said as they drove higher up into the hills.

The huge homes were built in isolated little pockets along secluded ravines and hilltops. The effect was privacy and the illusion of country living, even though the houses were really quite close to each other. Each house had a perfect, unobstructed view of the Pacific Ocean with nothing more than the slightest glimpse of a neighbor's roof to intrude. The maze of obscure lanes and private drives made their search more complicated.

This is going to be more of a challenge than I anticipated, Mark thought.

Tim drove up and down, and in and out of the gravel lanes. Beginning to feel a bit discouraged, they turned up a long driveway that clearly showed signs of neglect. The concrete was cracked, the weeds overgrown and the trees and shrubs had not been trimmed for a long time. Suddenly, Mark straightened up.

"Look, Tim, there's a No Trespassing sign and a No Hunting sign." His voice was tense with excitement. "This could be it."

"Let's not jump the gun, Padre. Let's take a little look see."

Getting out of the car, they approached the front door of the two-story house. Signs of neglect and deterioration were everywhere. Two-by-fours barred the entrance. The windows were impossible to see through thanks to several years of grime on the panes plus filthy drapes hanging inside.

Without a word, they walked around to the rear of the house and tried the door only to find it locked. Walking around the house, they tried several windows and the garage doors.

"Bingo!" Tim called out. Mark came running from the other side of the house and found Tim standing beside an open window.

"Wait by the door. I'll climb in and try to get it open for you."

"No, I'm right behind you, Tim."

They stood in the dark room letting their eyes adjust to gloom after the bright sunshine. There was no doubt they were in the right house.

"Would you look at this? No innocent children playing boogie men did this." Tim pointed to a wall covered with a large painting of a goat-headed devil complete with cloven hoofs and glowing red eyes. Not too far away was the all too familiar drawing of the amulet of the Kinghts Templar.

As their eyes adjusted to the gloom, their attention was drawn to the center of the room. There, covering the majority of the floor, was a large black circle surrounding a five-pointed star painted in blood red---a pentagram, also known as Satan's star, with two points up and one down to represent Satan's horns and his beard.

"You're right, this must be the place." Mark wrinkled his nose. "What is that disgusting smell?"

Tim didn't answer. Instead, his eyes turned to the middle of the pentagram. There, lying in the center was a black mound that seemed to be pulsating and squirming.
Mark stepped up to the ugly mass to study it. Upon closer examination, he discovered a congealed mass that was completely covered with flies. The constant buzzing and agitation of their feasting created an illusion of crawling movement. What had once been someone's beloved pet was now an ugly, stinking pile of rotting flesh.

The malodorous mass brought a sudden feeling of de'ja vu, a reminiscence of the nauseating stench of death that accompanied the removal of the dead mice under the house.

Bile rose up into Mark's throat and he covered his mouth and nose in an attempt to control his nausea. He rushed back to the window and leaned out, inhaling huge gulps of fresh air.

The veteran policeman still found it hard to look at such grisly sights, but for the dog-loving priest it was too much. After a few minutes and several gulps of air, Mark was reasonably certain that his breakfast would remain where it belonged, and he returned to Tim's side.

"Okay now?" Tim asked. Mark nodded.

"It's nothing to be ashamed of, you know. First couple of times I saw this filth, I couldn't eat for days."

Mark just shook his head from side to side. "I can't believe that kids could do this sort of thing. It's despicable and vile."

"It's television, Padre. Television and movies have made today's children heartless and numb to the suffering of others. They just don't seem to feel another's pain."

"But look at this. Don't you think it's a bit too sophisticated for teenagers?" Tim looked at the pentagram and back at Mark.

"What? The devil's star? Everyone today knows what that damn thing is," he replied.

"No, Tim, look at the walls." The priest pointed to a second wall that had been covered with a huge, hand-made calendar, covering the entire year. Highlighted were four dates. Tim walked over to the door and pushed it open to let in some sunlight.

With the light, more signs and symbols were revealed, but their attention was focused on the calendar. The four dates highlighted were the second day of February, the last day of April, the last day of July and the last day of October. Both men recognized the significance of the dates: Candlemas, Beltane, Lammas and Halloween.

"The four major witches' festivals," the priest observed.

"Just exactly how did they choose those particular days, Padre?"

"Witchcraft goes back a long way, Tim. All the way back to ancient periods in history when people worshipped nature. And each of these Sabbaths marks a turning point in the year when they believed magic was most potent. Candlemas, Beltane and Lammas are all very important dates chosen for their distinct phase of the 'tide cycle' of the witches' year."

He continued, "But Halloween is the most important of all the witches' holy days. It is the eve before November first, our Catholic All Saints' Day. It is their ancient feast of the dead and the last day of their year and happens to be the lowest point on the winter solstice. It is also the day when some Satanic cults are said to celebrate the Black Mass and offer human sacrifice. Each of these four days are also initiation dates for new members."

Mark stepped up to the calendar and pointed to the highlighted dates as he went on.

"Candlemas marks the end of the domain of darkness and renewal of life in nature. Beltane celebrates the awakening phase which happens to be the high point of summer. Lammas heralds the time of harvest and sweeps on until it joins the dark tide of Halloween. They worship the 'Mother Goddess' today as they did four thousand years ago…"

"Four thousand years?" Tim interrupted.

"Sure," the priest explained. "The ancient Druids, for instance, worshipped in forests and lonely meadows or glens. Today they still dress up in robes and practice their ancient rites in apartment complexes, large business offices and family recreation rooms. Shelby talked about robes, so I suspect this group is based on the Druids' religion rather than Gardnerian witchcraft," Mark continued.

"I'm impressed. You sure have done your homework." Tim said.

"Had to. It's necessary to know your enemy if you are going to beat him. What's our next step?"

Tim looked around the room. "I think, Father, that it is time to call in the local police. I'm really out of my jurisdiction here in Carmel. We'll need their help."

"Okay, let's go. This place gives me the willies."

As they left the room, Tim kicked the stub of a black candle as a parting shot. It rolled across the floor and stopped on the opposite side of the room, coming to rest at the base of the pentagram.

Chapter 13

Mom and Dad,
> Gone to take some books back to the school
> library. I'll be back soon. Don't worry, I'll
> be okay.

Shelby finished the note and left it on the kitchen counter where she knew her mother would find it. After the meeting with Father Ross and Lieutenant Bryant in the hospital, her parents had contacted Shelby's principal and explained as much of the situation as they could. They said they were taking Shelby out of school.

Her mother had gone into Monterey to arrange a leave of absence from her work at the Language School. Anne had made it clear she would stay with her daughter as long as Shelby was in danger.

Mike was at his office, setting the wheels in motion for Shelby's transfer to a private school on the East Coast. They had agreed upon a new school, far from the Monterey peninsula as the quickest and best solution to the danger that threatened her.

Shelby glanced at her watch---just a little past three. If she hurried she could still catch Mrs. Gallagher in the library. She might also be in time to say good-bye to some of her friends and teachers. In the warm sheltering arms of daylight, the terrors of the night seemed far away.

Driving her GEO Tracker along the picture-postcard lanes of the village, she was suddenly struck with the full impact of what was happening in her life. This place was home and she was being driven away from it by people she once trusted and called her friends. Tears of anger and betrayal welled up in her eyes. It was the first time in a long while she had felt any emotion other than fear.

Almost every home along Scenic Drive had a jack-o-lantern on display. In a few hours, their glowing faces would beckon to the innocent like a bright light bulb to a moth. Their leering grins seemed to mock the illusions she once cherished. The warm bubble of security that had enveloped her throughout her life had been burst and she doubted she would ever feel completely safe again.

The innocent fun of miniature ghosts and ghouls coming home now from their costume parties at school seemed somehow charged with something sinister. Halloween was no longer the happy time she remembered. Shelby now believed in monsters that went bump in the night.

A cat suddenly darted from underneath a hedge into Shelby's path. Slamming on the brakes just in time to avoid hitting it, she heard the squeal of brakes behind her. She looked in the rearview mirror and glimpsed the red Mustang. An explosion of fear jolted her body from head to toe.

****

Tossing his brief case into his car, Michael Townsend noticed some trick-or-treaters were already out, running from door to door with their bags. Looking at his watch, he was surprised to see that it was already after five. Slamming the car door closed, he wondered when this nightmare would end.

Pulling into the driveway, he noticed that Shelby's Jeep was not parked in its usual place. Neither was Anne's car in the garage. A sudden rush of fear stabbed Mike in the chest. His eyes zeroed in on the note lying on the counter as soon as he entered the kitchen. "Oh, no," he groaned. "Shelby, honey, why did you leave?" he said aloud to an empty house.

Mike ran back to his car not even bothering to lock the door. He jumped into his car and headed for the high school. He found himself praying for the first time in years.

"Please, God, let Shelby be there. Don't let anything happen to our baby. She's all we've got. Please, God."

As he came to the end of Scenic Drive, he could see just around the bend in the road. Shelby's Tracker was on the sandy shoulder along Ocean Avenue. Pulling up along side of the Jeep, it was obvious that Shelby was nowhere near and he could see a pile of school books lying on the seat.

****

Winding their way out of the densely forested hills of the Highlands, Tim and Mark turned north on Highway One and headed toward Carmel.

"I've been thinking," Mark began. "We can't just write these kids off. The more I think about it, the more uncomfortable I am with the prospect of leaving them to the likes of Marissa Bentley. We have to at least try to help them."

"What do you suggest? I've seen this sort of thing before and it never ends well for these kids."

"Why don't we start with Jeff Archer, Shelby's former boyfriend? How do you think his parents would react to a little pastoral visit on our part?"

"Who's to say that they aren't into this stuff themselves? I mean, these kids that we're dealing with are the children of the Sixties Generation, the flower children. I don't know if you've looked at your congregation lately, but I'll bet you won't find many of them gracing your pews. And their absence in Church doesn't necessarily mean that they've given up believing in something."

"I think I know what you mean. G.K. Chesterton wrote that when people give up their faith in God, the danger is not that they will believe in nothing, but that they will believe in anything."

Tim pulled into a convenience store parking lot and Mark walked over to a phone booth to check the telephone directory for the Archers' phone number and address. Mark dialed the number and introduced himself to the voice on the other end of the line."

"Hello."

"Hello, Mr. Ronald Archer?"

"Yes."

"I'm Father Mark Ross. I am the chaplain for the Benedictine Monastery just south of town. Do you have a teenaged son named Jeff?"

"Yes, I do. Is there anything wrong? What's this all about?" he asked with a tone of suspicion.

"I wonder, Mr. Archer, would it be convenient for you if I stop by and talk to you and your wife? I don't wish to alarm you, but your son may be in trouble and he needs your help."

An uncomfortable silence on the other end of the line prompted Mark to ask, "Mr. Archer, are you there?"

"Yes, I'm still here. All right, Father. Do you know where we live?"

"Yes, I have your address. I can be there in ten minutes."

"Fine, we'll be expecting you."

The two friends drove to Carmel Meadows, a subdivision of neatly appointed homes just south of the village proper. Anywhere else it would be considered a middle-class neighborhood. Here in Carmel there were no middle-class neighborhoods.

They were met at the door of the modest stucco house by two very worried-looking and slightly hostile parents.

"I should tell you right away that we're not Catholics, so I would like to know what the connection is between you and our son," asked Ronald Archer.

"Let me introduce Lieutenant Tim Bryant of the San Francisco Police Department," said Mark. The look of annoyance on Archer's face was quickly replaced by fear.

"What's Jeff done?" asked Susan Archer, stepping in front of her husband.

"Please don't be upset. My visit is strictly unofficial," offered Tim.

"May we come in?" asked the priest.

"Oh, I'm sorry. Please do come in," Mr. Archer invited.

Once inside and seated, Mark began. "What I have to tell you will be very difficult for you to hear. Believe me, it's not our intention to cause you any grief, but we have reason to believe that your son is in serious trouble and we want to help."

Susan Archer interrupted, "I think we already know why you and Lieutenant Bryant are here, Father Ross." She looked silently at her husband. They held each other's gaze for several seconds, then nodded.

"Father Ross, Lieutenant, would you mind coming with us? There's something we want to show you." She got up from the sofa.

Mark and Tim followed the Archers down the hall toward a room at the back of the house.

"This is Jeff's room," said Susan as she swung open the door and reached in for the light switch.

The sight that greeted them sent a wave of revulsion through the priest that reached to his very soul. Above the bed, an oversized picture of a goat-like creature dominated the room. Its forehead was emblazoned with a bloody pentagram. Its glowing red eyes were hypnotic.

The windows were covered with black contact paper, blotting all light. There was a student desk in the corner draped with a black cloth that had been converted into a kind of altar.

Covering the surface of the altar were the burned stubs of candles and dried pools of melted wax.

Ronald Archer stepped past the others clustered in the doorway and pulled back a section of carpet from the middle of the floor, revealing a red pentagram about six feet in diameter."

"A year ago, this was a typical high school kid's room---nothing but basketball trophies, bar bells and posters of 'Bay Watch' babes," he said, letting the carpet fall back in place.

"We've tried talking to him, even got him into counseling for awhile. He went a few times until the counselor told us that a certain amount of rebellion was natural for a boy Jeff's age and that we needed to respect his search to clarify his own value system. He told us that we should set limits but we should also allow Jeff his personal space and not intrude by violating the privacy of his room." Susan was close to tears as she spoke.

"You can imagine how we felt when we found all this," Ronald Archer joined in. "We're not religious people, but believe me, we're not into this stuff. It's sick. We even tried having a local pastor talk to Jeff, but it was like talking to a stone. He just wouldn't open up," said the distraught father. "To be honest, I don't think the pastor knew how to help. He seemed to be in over his head."

"We're so afraid that Jeff is slipping away from us and we don't know what to do about it." Susan cried as she put her arm around her husband.

Tim finally spoke, "I'm afraid it maybe even worse than you imagine. Let's go into the living room. I have something to tell you."

****

Shelby's heart seemed to explode in her chest when she saw Jeff's red Mustang in her rear view mirror. She tried to hold her car steady, but her hands were wet with perspiration. Gripping the steering wheel, she stepped down hard on the accelerator. She knew she had to get away from Jeff, but where? It was too far to the school and she knew her folks were not home yet. Father Mark was her best hope.

Her speed was too great for the winding curves of Scenic Drive and as she tried to make the turn onto Ocean Avenue, she lost control and the Jeep slid off the road into the soft sand.

Shelby pressed the accelerator, but the wheels just spun helplessly in the white powder.

Suddenly Jeff was outside her window. He pulled open the door and grabbed her arm.

"No, Jeff," she screamed. But the wind and waves were louder than her frightened voice.

"I just want to talk to you, Shell." There was a vulnerability in his pleading.

"I can't, Jeff. My parents are waiting for me. I have to get back home."

"You're going in the wrong direction if you're on your way home," the boy answered. "Come on, Shelby, just let me drive you home and we can talk."

"I don't think so, Jeff," she tried to pull her arm free.

"Come on, Shelby," Jeff cajoled, continuing to tug on her arm. Shelby tried to pull free but the athletic teenager was too strong for her. Realizing that his charm had failed, he grew impatient.

His whole demeanor changed instantly and he yanked her from her seat and threw her onto the sand. Not wanting to be seen by a passing car, he threw the full weight of his body on top of Shelby, knocking the wind from her. Before she could gather her wits, he dragged her through the sand and shoved her into the front seat of the Mustang, slamming the door. Before she could get out again, Jeff had run around to the driver's side and jumped into the car.

Jeff gunned the engine and laid rubber tire marks along the road as he headed out of town. Shelby screamed and tried to open the door. With one hand on the steering wheel, Jeff grabbed her with his free hand, slamming her head against the window.

Pain flashed through her head and she tried to lift her hand to her head, but it seemed too heavy. She realized she was losing consciousness and she fought to hold on.

"I tried to warn you, Shelby, but you wouldn't listen. We could have had it all. Anything we wanted we could have for the asking. The Master takes care of his own. But no---you had to turn chicken on us. Now look where you've gone and gotten us."

He was rambling, sucking in deep gulps of air. "I didn't want to hurt you or that priest, but I had to do what was necessary. I've always done what I had to do. That's what separates the weak from the strong...the leader from the sheep."

"Jeff, don't you see what you're doing? What you are becoming?" Shelby cried. "How could you do that to Miss Wayland? She was our friend. And Father Mark was only trying to help me."

"Shut up!" he shouted. "It's all your fault. No one would have been hurt if you had kept your mouth shut."

"I wanted to help you, Jeff," she cried. "You don't know what you've gotten yourself into. It's evil, Jeff."

"And I suppose you do?" he snarled. "It's power, Shell. The power to have anything you want in this world. Real power. I've seen it, Shell. Not the pie-in-the-sky your priest is preaching. Even Jesus called Satan the Prince of this world."

"Jeff, don't you see what's happening to you all? You're all selling your soul to the devil and what for? A car? A basketball trophy? It's not worth it. His promises are nothing but lies. Come with me, Jeff. We'll go to Father Mark. He will help us."

"It's too late for that, Shell. I wouldn't want to go back, even if I could," he said. You belong to him too, whether you want to admit it or not."

"Never!" She began to scream for help, reaching for the door handle.

"Shut up!" he yelled. Like a rocket his fist shot across the car, slamming her head into the window again. As she slumped in the seat and consciousness ebbed away, she heard Jeff's voice as if in an echo chamber.

"You can't leave now, Shell. You're our guest of honor tonight."

****

It was already late afternoon when Mark and Tim pulled up to the Chaplain's cottage. Michael Townsend was waiting for them. Jumping out of the parked car, he rushed over to them, saying, "They've got Shelby!"

Mark suddenly felt a spasm of pain in the pit of his stomach and a shortness of breath as if he'd been physically punched. Trying to keep his voice calm, he said, "Are you sure? Maybe she is saying good-bye to a friend."

"No, she was going to the school, but she never got there. Her car is on the side of the road at Ocean and Scenic. I found it there. Her books and jacket are on the seat. That was hours ago. I've looked everywhere for her."

The distraught father was beside himself. "The car was still running. I tried all of her friends, but no one has seen her."

Frantically running his fingers through his hair, Michael Townsend looked like a wild man. He pounded his fist on the hood of Tim's car. "What am I going to do?

"Where is Anne?" Tim asked.

"I called her at the Language School and told her that Shelby was gone. She's going crazy. What am I going to tell her?" Mike asked.

"Don't panic," Tim said. "We're going to find her, I promise. I think our first step is to get back to the police. Maybe they will listen to us now."

"Let's go inside and give them another call," Mark suggested as he led the way to the front door.

Pinned to the screen door was a folded rectangular piece of paper. Retrieving the note, Mark read the message aloud to the two men.

"Was visiting Mother Benedicta when Sister Paula came in with a box of groceries for you. I offered to drop them off. The door was unlocked so I left them on the kitchen counter. Sorry I missed you. Chloe.

P.S. Forgive me, Father, for I have sinned. I stole a loaf of Sister Paula's bread from your bundle. Hope you don't mind."

Reaching for the phone, Tim noticed the blinking red light signaling a waiting message.

"Mark, there's a message here for you." Depressing the button, the three men were stunned to hear the disembodied voice of Marissa Bentley.

"Father Ross, this is Marissa Bentley. After our meeting at the Pine Inn last night, I think it's time we talked, don't you? Thinking over what you said, I realize that you are under the impression that I am the locus of evil here on the peninsula. We may not agree with each other and we don't like each other, that is a given. But I am not the person you seem to think I am. However, I think I know who it is that you are really looking for."

The message continued. "I may be a pagan, to use your word, but I am not a Satanist, and I don't get involved with the dark side of the craft. I do, however, know my clients, and it doesn't take a great deal of detective work to know who is doing what. I think you'd be surprised to learn who some of my best customers are. Meet me here at my shop after closing time if you want to know more."

"What now?" frustration and fear put a demanding edge to Mike Townsend's voice. "Is everyone in this town involved in this hell."

"Take it easy," Tim spoke up. "We want to find Shelby, too, but we can't go off half cocked. We have to work together."

"I'm just scared out of my mind."

"I know, Mike. We are, too." Mark glanced at his watch as he spoke. "Tim, you go ahead and call the police. You may be able to get them to take us seriously. Mike, you stay with him. The police may want to talk to you personally. I'll head over to the bookstore and see what Miss Bentley has to say."

"Wait a minute, Mark." Tim said. I don't trust her. This could be some sort of trap or she may be trying to get you off the scent. I'd better come along as a witness just in case. Mike, you can go ahead and call the police. Use my name and tell them I'll get with them as soon as we check out Bentley."

Leaden clouds were rolling ominously over the horizon, stripping the sunset of its usual brilliance as the policeman and priest piled into the emerald green car. By the time they reached the village, it was twilight. All that remained of the dying day was a deep crimson gash slashed across the sky like a mortal wound.

Maneuvering the car into a parking space across the street from Crystal Visions, they sat silently in the idling car, looking at the store. The building was conspicuously dark, framed by the well-lit display windows of the two neighboring shops.

"She said to meet her here after closing," Mark said. It doesn't look like anyone is home."

"Let's take a closer look, it's not quite closing time. If it's locked we can always try the back door. There must be a rear exit to this place." Tim said as he climbed out of the small car.

"I don't know...suddenly I don't have a very good feeling about this, Tim."

"All of a sudden you're getting psychic on me," Tim said.

Exiting the car, they approached the darkened store. The door was closed and it appeared to be deserted.

"Come on," said Tim, trying the brass knob. The door swung open effortlessly. Entering the small shop, Mark called out, "Hello. Is anyone here?"

There was only silence.

"Why do you suppose she went out? And why did she leave the door unlocked? What kind of game is she playing? Watch your step, Mark---it's darker than a cave in here."

"I'm right behind you," the priest said. The tall street lamps behind them cast long shadows as they slipped into the darkened building. Darkness swallowed the two men as they inched forward.

Suddenly a horrible scream pierced the silence. Both men jumped back, hearts pounding like jack hammers."

"What in the hell was that?" Tim's question was answered when Marissa's cat howled again as it escaped through the open door, a black shadow streaking into the night.

"Damn that cat! I stepped on its tail. It scared the spit out of me." Mark caught his breath.

"Well, at least we know we are alone. That cat could wake the dead."

Except for the sound of the wind outside, all was still. The butterflies in Mark's stomach made him feel queasy and short of breath. He asked, "What are we looking for anyway? She's obviously not here?"

"I'm not sure yet. Just stay close. Something is not right here," Tim answered.

Moving deeper into the darkness, their eyes gradually adjusted to the gloom. Mark could make out the outlines of the bookshelves and curio cases lining the walls.

They advanced toward the darkest part of the room, farthest from the street lights spilling through the display window.

Mark could just barely make out the beaded curtain separating the shop from the back room. Suddenly his toe struck something solid, sending the object rolling across the floor with the sound of a small bowling ball. It came to a thudding halt against the wall four feet from where Mark stood.

He held his breath and waited.

He listened, but the only sound he heard was the wind wailing outside.

In the dim illumination of the halogen street lamps, Mark could make out the object where it had come to rest against the wall. Like a huge star sapphire, a pentacle of light reflected off the object, which seemed to be bathed in a liquid sheen. He bent down and retrieved the softball-sized sphere. It felt cold in his palm, but oddly sticky.

Tim was at his side. "What have you got there?"

"I'm not sure." Tim produced a miniscule pocket flashlight that doubled as a key ring. Pointing the tiny beam at the glassy orb, the object glowed in Mark's outstretched palm---a crystal ball streaked with a tacky, rust-colored smear.

"Blood?" asked Mark.

"And not very old from the look of it."

"Tim, I think maybe its time to call the police."

"Yeah, but first I want to look around. Ah, there's the light switch." As light flooded the shop it was plain to see that someone had ransacked the place. Books and paraphernalia had been swept from shelves and strewn everywhere.

"What's going on here?" Mark asked.

"Seems that someone was looking for something. The question is, did they find it?"

"Tim, the cash drawer is open. Someone robbed her."

"Looks like it, but where is Marissa?" Tim was speaking as he walked through the beaded curtain. "Oh, oh. Better stay out there, Padre."

"What do you see?" Mark rushed through the curtain, stumbling into something on the floor. Catching his balance, he looked down into the lifeless, staring eyes of Marissa Bentley.

Tim pushed past Mark and knelt down to check for a pulse, knowing already that it was useless. He gently closed her eyes. Marissa's dark hair was matted with congealing blood and her long fingernails were torn and broken as if she had tried to fight off her attacker. The coppery scent of blood was overwhelming. As any priest would, Mark knelt down beside the body and traced the sign of the cross over the still form, pronouncing words of conditional absolution.

"This was no robbery," Tim said. "Someone wanted us to think that."

"How can you tell, Tim? The money is missing from the cash drawer."

"She wouldn't risk her life and fight someone over a few dollars. The robbery was just a cover up. Someone knew you would be coming here and they couldn't have set you up better. Your fingerprints are all over that crystal ball and half of Carmel saw you and Marissa going at it in the Pine Inn last night."

Beyond the storefront windows, the last embers of daylight had been snuffed out. The gray twilight had surrendered, ceding to the inky blackness. A gaggle of howling trick-or-treaters ran past the store, shattering the stillness, transformed by their own imaginations into creatures of the night.

"I'll call the police and while I wait for them here---you get back to Mike. We don't have any time to waste. We need to find Shelby fast. And don't touch anything else in the store. Maybe the killer left a print or two that we haven't destroyed yet."

Mark pulled into the driveway leading to the chaplain's cottage. There was no sign of the police, but Mike was waiting for him. "Where are the police?" Mark asked as he jumped out of the car.

"They left! They just listened to me and left." The anxious father was becoming more frantic by the minute. "They acted like it was just a dumb Halloween prank. I was just about to leave."

"It's ok, Tim is with them by now at the bookstore. We found Marissa Bentley dead---murdered---so I guess its up to us now. Let's go. We'll take my car. It's darker and not as easy to spot in the moonlight as your silver BMW."

"All right, Father, just a minute. I think we may need this." Mike opened his car door and reached under the seat. Pulling out a pistol, he quickly joined Mark in the waiting car.

"I think I know where she might be," Mark said.

"What are we waiting for?" Mark punched the accelerator as the car sped out of the drive and turned south toward the Highlands.

****

Slowly, Shelby's awareness of her surroundings began to surface as she was being jostled back and forth. Jeff was taking turns at breakneck speed. Her head ached so badly that she didn't want to open her eyes. She felt the Mustang bump along a road full of potholes and she realized that they had left the smooth highway.

She forced her eyes open to see where they were, but the pain in her head and the darkness disoriented and confused her. With terror, she realized that her hands were tied and she was lying on the floor of Jeff's back seat.

Shelby tried to sit up, but the movement caused terrible pain in her hands. The pain shot up her arms and her fingers tingled from loss of blood. She wondered how long she had been tied up. Waves of nausea washed over her and she had a terrible metallic taste in her mouth.

"Jeff, where are we?"

"Sleeping Beauty is awake," Jeff snarled. "You've been out so long I thought you might miss your own party."

They were driving up the long, winding drive to the abandoned house.

"Please, Jeff, don't do this. Take me home. I won't tell anyone. I swear I won't. Please let me go."

"No! It's too late. You had your chance."

Tears of fear and frustration rolled down Shelby's face. Her mind was filled with a cold terror that overcame her ability to reason.

"Don't do this to me, Jeff," she continued to beg. "I'll do anything. My father will give you whatever you ask. Just let me go."

"Shut up!" he yelled. "I don't want to hear you." He reached across the seat and slapped her hard across the mouth with the back of his hand.

Shelby pressed up against the back door as far from her tormentor as she could get. She tasted blood and a warm trickle dribbled down her chin.

"I don't want to be a part of the circle, Jeff," she whined. "I told you I was through with the coven. I can't be a part of it anymore."

"Who said you are going to be part of the circle? You had your chance and you blew it. We didn't have any trouble replacing you. The world is divided between users and losers. You could have been one of us, but instead you chose to be a loser. But we're giving you one last chance to take part in a service. Tonight you are our guest of honor."

Even in the darkness, Shelby recognized the familiar twists and turns of the Highlands. For just one instant she glimpsed the dilapidated two-story house before Jeff dimmed the headlights and pulled up the cracked, crumbling driveway.

There were several other vehicles already parked behind the house. Shelby recognized some of them from the school's student parking lot. Jeff got out and walked around to open her door.

He dragged her out and started to push her towards the house. She tried to pull away, but her legs were too weak and asleep from the prolonged position of being curled up on the car floor. She fell. Jeff yanked her up and pushed her forward. She struggled to pull free, but the more she struggled, the tighter he gripped her.

"Jeff, you're hurting me," she cried.

"Then stop fighting. They're waiting for us." He turned her around and began dragging her back toward the house. Nearing the house, Shelby could hear the familiar chanting.

"No, Jeff, no. Please don't do this to me."

Reaching the door, he pulled her inside. She knew that screaming would do no good---the house was too far from neighboring homes. But all reason had been driven from her mind and Shelby screamed and screamed.

Several robed figures broke away from the circle to assist Jeff. Shelby fainted as the figures closed in.

Chapter 14

The speeding car pulled off Highway One and headed up the road behind the Highland Inn.

"Can't this thing go any faster?" Mike asked.

"We won't be any help to Shelby if we run off the road," Mark said.

"Sorry. You're right, Padre." Mike Townsend used Tim's familiar nickname for the priest. "I'm just so damned scared. Lord knows what is happening to her."

"I don't want to frighten you any more than you already are---I think that we turn left here." Mark interrupted himself.

"I think she'll be safe until midnight."

"Why midnight, Father?" the frantic man asked.

"That's the time, from midnight to three a.m.--- when witches and Satanists celebrate their Black Mass. Sort of a mockery of the three hours that Jesus hung on the cross. He was crucified at noon and expired at three p.m. Everything they do is directly opposite of what we do when we re-enact the sacrifice on Calvary with our Mass." Mark paused. "Mike, watch for a small road coming up on your right."

"Ok, Father," Mike answered. "I see it." The little car handled amazingly well on the winding roads as he pulled off onto the smaller road and continued climbing up the mountainside past houses lit up for trick-or-treaters. Smiling jack-o'-lanterns welcomed little ghosts and pirates running from house to house with sacks of candy.

What a mockery, Mark thought. We play with evil from early childhood, dressing up as witches and monsters and making games of Ouija Boards and crystal balls. Is it any wonder that these youngsters were so vulnerable.

The car continued to climb, until Mark said, "Here we are." He slowed down. "I think it would be best if we pull off the road here and hike in."

"Where?" Mike asked. "I can't see a damn thing out there. Are you sure we're at the right place?"

"Yeah, I'm sure. The windows are covered and the house sits pretty far back, but this is the place."

"Well, let's go." Mike was out and running before Mark could stop him.

"Hold it, Mike!" Mark called. "Take it easy. Don't let them know we are here. It would be better if we take them by surprise."

With no street lights to guide them, the night seemed preternaturally dark. It took a minute or two for their eyes to adjust to the blackness as they hurried toward the house, stumbling in the dark.

The moon slid out from behind a cloud momentarily, illuminating the house and several cars parked around it. Just before the moon disappeared behind another cloud, Mike recognized the red Mustang.

"That's Jeff Archer's car," he whispered.

"I'm sure that's the same car that ran me off the road," Mark whispered.

Stealthily, the two men approached the house. Drawing nearer, they could hear the muffled sound of chanting. Several voices blending into one, lifeless monotone, "As above, so below. As above, so below." Over and over.

"What are they doing?" Mike whispered. In spite of the cool evening, his face was glazed with sweat.

"They are putting themselves into a trance," Mark replied in a low voice. They crept up to a window that had been covered from inside with an old blanket. Along the sides there were narrow strips of light escaping where the blanket didn't quite reach.

Huddled against the house, both men peered inside. Scores of candles glimmered around the room, creating a yellow glow.

Around the pentagram on the floor sat a dozen hooded figures cross-legged and swaying from side to side in unison.

The chant had somehow changed to numbers. "Nine, nine, nine," they repeated nine times. "Eight, eight, eight," was chanted in the same monotone eight times.

There was something almost hypnotic in the chant. Mark grabbed Mike's arm and whispered, "I don't see her. Let's try another window." Mike nodded, following Mark as he led the way around to the back side of the house. They found a window with a better view. The material covering it was too small and left open a wider space. Again, they took their positions alongside one another.

"Oh, my God!" Mike blurted.

"Don't give us away," Mark warned. Both men had seen Shelby at the same time, when one of the chanters had swayed a little too far, opening a gap between himself and the hooded figure next to him.

Shelby was lying naked on the floor in the center of the pentagram. Her hands and feet were tied and a wide strip of tape covered the lower half of her face. She was struggling with her bonds, pulling and tugging, to no avail. Her eyes were wide with terror and her face was wet with tears. Mark put his hand on Mike's arm.

"Hold on. Let's wait for Tim and the police."

"No! I'm going in there. That's my daughter." Mark held Mike's arm in a vise grip, trying to hold him back.

Before either man could do anything, the circle of worshipers suddenly parted, forming two rows facing each other across the pentagram. A figure in red could clearly be seen now standing above Shelby's head. In a commanding, but obviously feminine voice, she began to recite her dark litany.

"Listen to the words of the Great Mother, who was called among men: Astarte, Artemis, Diana, Aphrodite, Arianrod, Cerridween. I am her vessel, I am her voice. Harken to the secrets of the craft, to be naked in your rites and to sing, dance and worship."

"Hail Satan!" answered the swaying congregation.

"I who am the beauty of the green earth and the white amongst the stars, and the mystery of the waters, and the secret desires of men's hearts, call thee unto thy servants; arise and come to me."

"Hail Satan!"

Two black-robed figures stepped forward and took up position on either side of the terrified girl. On command from the crimsoned-robed priestess, they knelt and kissed Shelby's naked breasts. There was something almost mechanical in their motions, devoid of any eroticism.

A wave of revulsion washed over the priest. But it was blind rage that took hold of Mike Townsend as he struggled against Mark's restraining grip.

"No, Mike, stop! Don't look. Tim can't be far behind. With or without the police, I know he'll be here.

We can't move without help. There's too many of them. We need help if we are going to save her."

The two men continued to watch in horror as the obscene Sabbath progressed. The veiled priestess began her procession around the circle, moving three times to the left and then three times to the right. She continued her litany to the Dark Power.

"Prince of Darkness."

"Hail Satan!" the figures responded.

"Lord of the Underworld."

"Hail Satan!"

"Leveler of Scores."

"Hail Satan!"

"Our True God."

"Hail Satan!"

"Lord of the Dispossessed."

"Hail Satan!"

The congregation's chanting had changed now. Swaying back and forth on their feet, their voices grew louder and louder, as they became oblivious to their surroundings or fear of discovery. Their mounting excitement was audible now in the intensity of their droning. "Hail Satan! Hail Satan! Hail Satan!"

Both Mark and Mike sensed immediately that the Black Sabbath was moving toward some hideous climax.

"Jesus, save us," prayed Mark silently. "God, please help us, help us. Holy Mary, Mother of God, pray for us." His pleading dissolved into formulas he had learned in his childhood. "Hail Mary, full of grace, the Lord is with Thee. Blessed are thou among women, and blessed is the fruit of thy womb, Jesus."

Several of the robed worshipers moaned in a rush of uninhibited rapture. Shelby struggled against the leather thongs that pinned her to the floor. Again and again she tried to scream but with the tape over her mouth, she was only able to produce a sound resembling that of a strangled animal. Unable to speak, she tossed her head wildly from side to side, pleading with her eyes for mercy. But her persecutors were beyond mercy, beyond fear.

Shelby's terrified stare fixed on the red robe moving closer to her head. Her eyes widened in horror as the high priestess produced a long, tapered dagger from the folds of her sleeve. The burnished blade caught the glint of black candles as she raised it skyward, beginning an incantation to enlist the Powers of Darkness.

From his hiding place outside the room, Mark recognized the dagger as the Athame, the magic knife of the Witches' Sabbath. Suddenly realizing with horror what the last act of this vile drama would be, Mark tried to stand but found himself frozen in place.

His heart pounded in his throat. The world spun in nightmarish circles around him. It was as if he were paralyzed---his limbs chained by some superior force. The world around him shifted into slow motion. He felt as if he were watching the events around him from the bottom of a swimming pool with a million gallons of water between him and the surface. A crushing weight bore down upon him, smothering his senses and holding him fast. He couldn't even open his mouth to let Mike know he was in trouble.

They were out of time. He had to act now. God give me strength, he prayed desperately. With all of his concentration, Mark focused every ounce of strength on his right arm. "God help me." He pushed with all his might.

Like a crack in a dam, a tiny trickle became a roaring flood as his strength surged back. The unearthly chains snapped. He lurched to his feet, pulling Mike up with him.

With lightening speed, they raced to the back door. Mark felt his grip on Mike's arm slip as Townsend fell with a sickening crack, tripping over a loose brick in the back steps.

Michael cursed in pain, grabbing his ankle and drawing his knee up to his chest. "Go on, Father, hurry!" Please hurry! For God's sake."

Mark reached the door and hurled his body against it. The rotten wood splintered as the door burst open, hanging lopsided on one hinge. Thirteen faces turned in unison as he fell through the doorway, landing in a crumpled heap.

Screams of outrage and surprise erupted as the circle dissolved into mad confusion. In a crazed flurry of black robes, hooded figures scrambled in all directions. Mark tried to reach the red-robed assassin before the deadly blade found its target.

One of the circle lunged forward in an attempt to block Mark's advance. Mark tried to sidestep the tackle, but felt the air knocked out of him as the young, muscular body slammed into him.

In the few seconds it took Mark and his attacker to tumble to the floor, the panicked congregation realized that no one else had followed him through the shattered portal. Becoming aware that they had only the lone priest to contend with, their courage quickly returned to them and they began to regroup. Shrieking like a dangerously wounded animal, they descended en masse on the dazed priest.

"Kill him! He has defiled the Sabbath," screamed the high priestess. The blows and kicks from a dozen fists and feet fell upon any part of Mark's body not covered by the beefy frame lying on top of him.

All at once, a deafening crack split the air reverberating through the room. The howling mob went silent. Mark lowered the protecting shield of his hands and saw Michael Townsend leaning in the shattered door frame, holding aloft a smoking Glock .45.

Blood oozed from a deep gash above his eye. It was as if Mark were looking at a freeze frame from a horror movie. The frenzied figures stood like statues.

"Nobody move!" shouted Mike, aiming the pistol at the crowd. "I swear to God, I'll blow away any one of you bastards that so much as twitches!"

Mark seized the moment and brought his knee up sharply into his attacker's stomach. The body on top of him doubled up in a spasm of pain and Mark rolled over until they had changed positions. Mark rammed his fist into the hood, making painful connection with flesh and bone.

Roughly yanking back the hood, he found himself staring into the face of Jeff Archer. His handsome face was a bloodied, contorted mask of evil and anger. He struggled to rise and Mark punched the husky teenager again. Blood splattered from his broken nose and Archer went down to the floor like a rock.

Struggling to his feet, Mark could hear police sirens screaming in the distance. The scarlet figure stood over the prone girl holding the blade aloft---poised for the kill.

Mark's heart was pounding in his ears and adrenalin was rushing through his veins as he tried to reach the dagger before it could plunge into the terrified girl.

Mike fired off another round, drawing the scarlet priestess's attention away from Shelby for a split second. It was all the time Mark needed to close the distance. He careened into his target. They crashed to the floor in a tangle of arms and legs, rolling like a crimson tumbleweed as the red velvet gown became a web engulfing both of them. Thrashing about the floor, they knocked over a candelabra, which sent flaming streams of molten wax across the room.

At that moment, the crumbling wood of the door frame gave way under Mike Townsend's weight and he went crashing to the floor. Seizing the opportunity for escape, the demonic disciples fled in all directions.

A hot flash of pain suddenly seared through Mark's shoulder and down his arm as the dagger plunged into his flesh. The shock caused him to loosen his grip on his squirming opponent. With amazing speed, his adversary twisted free and was on her feet running. Before Mark could regain his footing, the sorceress sprinted across the room and crashed through one of the blanketed windows escaping into the night.

Mark charged to the window in pursuit. He leaned against the windowsill and felt the broken shards of glass crunch beneath his palms. The knife wound in his shoulder throbbed with pain. Looking out into the darkness, he strained to glimpse some movement, some shadow that would betray the location of his opponent. He saw nothing but the silently swaying trees silhouetted in the pale moonlight.

Mark could feel the blood running down his arm now. The shock was beginning to wear off. He was aware of a growing patch of cold dampness around his shoulder as the cool autumn air rushed in from outside. Suddenly his attention shifted to the right---toward the driveway---as he continued to search the darkness.

In the dim light, a pandemonium of shadows raced toward the parked cars around the back of the house. Without their leader, the coven had dissolved into an undisciplined mob running helter-skelter to escape.

Arms flaying, hands wildly tearing at their robes, pushing and shoving, tripping and falling, becoming entangled.

Car doors were yanked open and ignitions flared into life as the fleeing cultists tried to make good their escape. But it was too late.

A speeding caravan of flashing blue and red lights was rapidly winding its way through the twists and curves of the Highlands---Tim's black limo in the lead. Before the first pick-up could escape, the police cruisers had cut off their retreat. Relief poured over Mark as he watched the police round up most of the coven.

Tim entered the house with three Carmel officers.

"Looks like we missed most of the action," he said as he hurried over to Mark.

"Tim, the leader got away!" Mark shouted. "Come on! We can still get her."

"Don't worry, Padre, we've got enough of the kids here. They'll give us the names of the ones that got away.

If not, the DMV can identify them by their plates. There's several cars out there with no drivers."

Just then they were interrupted by the sounds of a struggle taking place behind them. Turning toward the shattered doorway, they were greeted with the sight of two Monterey County Sheriff's deputies flanking a crimson-clad figure who squirmed and twisted in their grasp.

"Here's one that didn't get away," the first one said.

"And this one's a little too old to be playing trick or treat."

The two officers were half-dragging, half-carrying their cloaked prisoner, who fought and struggled like an animal caught in a trap.

"She tried to make her getaway through the woods."

Tim approached the writhing captive as she tried vainly to twist free of the deputies' grip. With a deft motion, he pulled back the cowl obscuring her face.

Like a Salvador Dali painting, Mark's world suddenly went surreal. The planet itself seemed to shift beneath his feet. Absolute shock shot through Mark as he found himself staring into the wild eyes of his old friend. "Chloe! Why? How? But you can't be!" he stammered. "How?" His words ran together with a torrent of pain, betrayal and disbelief registering on his face.

Her frantic, darting eyes focused on him for a moment, and the frightened animal look was replaced with a hateful glare of such pure malevolence that Mark almost gasped aloud.

"I don't understand," he pleaded. The sadness and gentle quality of his voice only seemed to heighten the malignity staring back at him.

"You really don't understand anything, do you, dear boy. Always so confident. Always so sure of your dogmas---as if the truth were your own personal property that you graciously dispensed to the great unwashed. You and your fellow priests. I think that's what I hated about you the most---your arrogant belief in the absolute rightness of your own convictions. The gospel according to Mark---Mark Ross."

Mark continued to stare, dumbfounded, as Chloe twisted and turned trying in a vain effort to pull free of the officers' restraints. "You're wondering why I did it. Well, where was your God of mercy and goodness when my husband was blown into bloody bits in Korea? Where was He when I was left alone without a husband, without a child? I'll tell you, He was nowhere. He's powerless. He's a fraud. And so are you, priest, and all your kind."

"Chloe, I can't believe this. What are you saying?" the startled priest asked.

"I'm saying, I took control of my own life, my own destiny. I learned from Shamen in Africa and witch doctors in Haiti. I studied the occult, I studied wicca and I learned to bend the Powers of Darkness to my will! My will!" she shrieked.

"Chloe, you've been a practicing Catholic for as long as I've known you. You're a lay minister of the Eucharist, we trusted you to visit the sick and take Holy Communion to them. Didn't that mean anything to you?"

"Yes, it meant something to me. It meant I had an unending supply of consecrated hosts for my Sabbaths."

"But, Chloe, what did you hope to gain by losing your soul to Satan?"

"Power! You stupid, simpering, overgrown altar boy. Even your Bible calls Satan 'the lord of this world'. I chose to stand under his banner. I'm on the winning side, Priest. Don't you look so smug," she sneered. The police officer pulled Chloe towards the waiting cruiser.

"We're not finished yet," she screamed. "Not finished yet."

Tim was at Mark's side, resting his hand on his friend's shoulder.

"There will be time enough for questions later, Mark. Right now we have other things to take care of. The two men turned to face Michael and Shelby. Father and daughter were huddled together in a tight embrace. He had wrapped his jacket around her, cradling her in his arms as they gently rocked back and forth. It was obvious that Mike was trying to balance on his one good leg.

"Thank you, thank you both. I owe you my daughter's life." His voice cracked with emotion. "She would be dead now if not for you, Father." Tears were rolling unashamedly down his face.

"How can I ever thank you? What can I say?"

"You don't have to say anything, Mike." Mark answered. "Besides, you were pretty handy yourself. If you hadn't come along when you did, both Shelby and I would be dead now."

"Mike, you need to get to the hospital," Tim ordered. "A doctor should see to that ankle as soon as possible. Let a cruiser take you and Shelby now and I'll call your wife. She can meet you at the hospital." He glanced at the girl.

"Shelby's had about all she can take for one night. We can get her statement tomorrow." Tim recognized the need to get Shelby away from this place.

"We'll clear it with the police. And we know where to find you if we need to. Come on, I'll help you to a car."

Mike turned once more to Mark, reaching out to shake his hand. As Mark lifted his hand, a white hot blast of pain surged through his arm, leaving him dizzy. The room spun and he stumbled and went down, his right knee connecting sharply with the floor.

"Slow down, Mark. Let me take a look at that shoulder of yours. Tim was on his knees, gently pulling Mark's sweater over his head, trying not to cause his friend any pain.

"We've got to get you to the hospital, too. This shoulder looks bad." Tim put his jacket carefully over Mark's shoulders and helped him to his feet. Putting his arm around Mark to steady him, they walked together to Tim's limo.

"You're going to the hospital in style, Padre."

As they watched Mike drive off with Shelby in the back of a patrol car, Mark said a silent prayer of thanksgiving. It was colder now and much darker. A high-pitched whine could be heard as the ocean breeze blew through the pine forest with gathering force.

The two friends started down the hillside in Tim's long, black car. The burned out jack-o'-lanterns were no longer smiling. The last of the trick-or-treaters had long since gone home to open their sacks of candy and be tucked safely in their beds.

Halloween this year had come to an end. It was one Halloween that both men would remember for as long as they lived.

EPILOGUE

San Francisco

Six Months Later

"Telephone call for you, Father. It's your policeman friend, I think." Tony Malatesta, the custodian of St. Philip's Church, stuck his head into the sacristy where Father Mark was vesting for Mass.

The Maltese caretaker's accent always reminded Mark of Count Dracula. The priest glanced at the clock above the cabinet. He had a good fifteen minutes before Mass was to begin, enough time to take Tim's call.

Mark slipped the chasuble over his head. "I'll be right there, Tony."

Entering the rectory by way of the dark narrow breezeway that connected it to the Church, he went to his office on the first floor and picked up the phone.

"Top of the morning to you, Officer."

"And the rest of the day to you, Padre," Tim answered in his best Irish brogue.

"What's up?" Mark asked.

"What are you doing after Mass? How would you like to take a little drive down the coast to Monterey with me?" Tim said.

"I think I could manage that," Mark answered.

"Good. I got word that the final hearing is set for eleven this morning. Thought you might want to be there."

Four p.m. that same day

"Praised be Jesus Christ..." The wooden shutters of the speak-room slid back with a clacking noise revealing the grinning face of Mother Benedicta.

"Now and forever," answered Mark and Tim in unison.

"So nice to see you both. The sisters miss you and your homilies, Father." Mother Benedicta took her chair. "I take it you have just come from the hearing in Monterey?"

"You never cease to amaze me, Mother." Tim smiled.

"Oh, my glory! Lieutenant. We may be behind bars, but we really do try to keep abreast of what is happening outside our gates. You know what they say about being in the world, but not of it. I'm sure Father Ross could tell you what the mission of a monastery is. Sooner or later all the pain of the world flows through our gates in the form of requests for prayers."

She continued, " And believe me, we've been doing a lot of praying for these poor youngsters. So many families here have been touched by this terrible thing. I've always wondered why this case has never been brought to trial."

"Oh, it's really not surprising, Mother. These cases seldom are," Tim said. Somewhere deep within the recesses of the monastery a door slammed, echoing through the polished corridors.

Tim went on, "Since we were dealing with minors, it was unlikely that they'd do jail time. Instead, in a series of hearings, the court chose to extend its jurisdiction over the kids and then remand them into the custody of their parents with mandatory counseling for the next two years."

Mark broke in, "The way the court looks at it, the teens were victims of Chloe's evil influence. And since they are minors, the judge chose to take a more lenient path."

"But what about poor Miss Wayland, Shelby's teacher?" asked the nun.

"Under questioning, the youngsters were unanimous in saying that they only meant to scare Janet that evening, not kill her," explained Tim. "Their stories have been confirmed in the counseling sessions. Janet Wayland's death has been ruled as an accident. The autopsy is consistent with that hypothesis."

A look of deep sadness overshadowed the Mother Superior's face as she shook her head slowly. "What a strange chain of unhappiness and deceit."

"And it goes on, Mother," Mark said. "Do you remember my telling you about Stacy Ballard, the girl in black? Chloe's protégé?"

"Yes, Father. She seemed to me to be the most troubled of all the children from what I read in the papers."

"She really was. The night of the raid she was so disturbed that she couldn't be kept with the others. In fact, she spent three days in Mt. Zion's Psychiatric Ward. She is now being institutionalized at Atascadero."

"Oh dear, that poor child. We will pray for her, Father. Do they have any hope for her recovery?"

"Mother, she is living in another world. I've been to see her several times, " Mark replied. "I know this may sound medieval, but I've come to wonder if some of those in mental hospitals are truly insane or in fact possessed. I

187

look into that girl's eyes and I see evil staring back at me. So far she has been unresponsive to conventional therapy. She has taken to signing her letters 'Asteroth'."

"Asteroth?" Mother questioned.

"A high ranking demon in the hierarchy of hell, Mother."

"Father, do you think an exorcism is in order?"

"Well, that would depend on whether the girl's parents requested one. And you know how long and involved the procedures are for determining the need for one."

"I will begin a novena to St. Michael this very night," Mother said. "But on a happier note, I received a lovely letter from Shelby."

"So have Tim and I," Mark replied. "She seems to be doing very well at her new school. Her parents say she is happier and making friends left and right."

"Shelby's a very lucky girl," Tim said. "God knows where she would be today if she hadn't had the courage to stand up against them. I hate to think what might have happened if she hadn't gone to Father Mark."

"Yes, Lieutenant Bryant, God is good. And you, Father, how is your shoulder?"

"Good as new, Mother."

"What about Chloe? Is there any news of her?"

"I've tried several times to see her, but she refuses to meet with me. Even prisoners have the right to refuse visitors. However, I have been able to learn that she has been involved in the occult for quite some time---probably as far back as my student days at Berkeley."

Father continued, "Apparently there has been a very active coven right here in Carmel since the twenties. It would seem that there is an underground network of covens across the country, maybe even across the world as far as we know. They're all aware of each other's existence. That's why Chloe retired in Carmel after leaving Berkeley. It seems that the members have been dying off for decades. That was why she was sent down here, to breathe new life into the coven. It was her idea to recruit new members from the high school. Her volunteer work at the school provided her with a perfect cover."

"And what of Ms. Bentley? Was she in the coven, too?"

"No, oddly enough, she wasn't. But she did know who was. She knew enough about the occult to understand why some of her customers were ordering certain materials. I think that was why she called me the night she was killed. She had recognized some of her clients at Mass that Sunday she visited the Monastery Chapel. Chloe probably heard her message on my answering machine when she was delivering groceries at the cottage. The police are convinced that she killed Marissa to keep her from talking."

"Do you think she really would have killed that poor child?"

"I do. It would have solidified her hold over the other youngsters by making them accomplices to murder."

"Well, I am certainly glad to see the end of this terrible affair."

"No more than I am, Mother, no more than I am," Mark sighed.

****

It was late in the evening by the time Tim's limousine pulled up in front of St. Philip's Rectory.

"I hope none of my parishioners are watching. They may get the idea that I'm living in the fast land if they see me getting out of a limo at this hour." Mark stepped out of the car.

"Just tell them the Archbishop drove you home," Tim said with a twinkle in his eyes. Mark stretched and looked up into the starry brilliance of the night sky. It was perfect, one of those evenings that made him fall in love with San Francisco all over again.

"Want to come in for a nightcap, Tim?"

"No, thanks. I'm sure Mary is still up and wondering where I am. You know, the cop's wife syndrome."

"You know, Counselor, I was thinking on the way home tonight that you and I have been through a lot together."

"We have indeed."

"But even now, there have been moments during these months when the memory of it all---Shelby, Marissa, Chloe and the rest---seemed to have an unreal quality about it. If it weren't for the scar on my shoulder, I could have convinced myself that it was all a bad dream."

"Well, if it's a dream, at least it has had a happy ending. Cheer up, Padre, this time the good guys won."

The two friends waved to each other and the long, black car pulled away from the curb, disappearing into the sultry spring night.

Mark turned away from the street and started up the low flight of steps to the rectory. At the top of the stoop, something curious caught his eye. In the warm yellow glow of the porch light was a package wrapped in brown paper and tied with string.

He picked it up. It was addressed to 'The Reverend Father Mark Ross'. There was no return address.

More of Mrs. Romitti's cannolis, he thought, placing the box under his arm as he fumbled for his house keys. This morning after Mass, she had said something about dropping some of the pastries off at the rectory later.

Tiptoeing through the darkened rectory so as not to awaken his confrere, Father Haley, Mark made his way to the kitchen. He would get inordinate delight in calling Tim tomorrow to let him know in mouth-watering detail what he had missed in not accepting his invitation for a nightcap.

Taking a scissors from a kitchen drawer, he snipped the twine from the parcel. Already salivating with anticipation, he tore away the brown paper and pulled the lid from the cardboard box.

At that moment a disheveled apparition materialized in the doorway. A groggy Father Pete Haley shuffled into the kitchen in his threadbare terry-cloth robe and slippers, so worn out that even the dog wouldn't be interested in them.

Yawning as he brushed a shock of white hair from his face, he squinted in the harshness of the neon light.

"I wondered what that noise was. Burning the midnight oil, Mark?" he said, more out of curiosity than reproach.

But his younger friend gave no response. He just continued to stare into the cardboard box in front of him, oblivious to the other man's presence. There was something about the way that Mark stood there, like a statue, every muscle in his body tense and frozen, that sent a sudden shiver of fear through Father Pete's heart. "What is it?"

For a moment Mark raised his eyes from the box and looked at his friend with an expression the older priest had never seen before.

Crossing the kitchen in four steps, Haley closed the distance between himself and Mark and peered over his shoulder.

He wasn't sure, at first, what exactly it was that he was seeing. White tissue paper was carefully arranged around something that was also white. It took a few seconds before he realized that he was staring at the headless, blood-drained bodies of two snow-white doves.

Send Crystal Visions to Your Friends

Look for "Children of the Crystal Vision" at your favorite bookstore. If you can't find it there, use this coupon to order:

Name_____

Address _____

City _____

State _____ Zip _____

Please send:

_____ copies at $12.95 each $ _____

(Californians, add 7% sales tax)   _____

Add Shipping and Handling   2.00

TOTAL $ _____

Make check or money order payable to Irisa Publishing.

Mail to: Irisa Publishing
          55 Marina Vista Avenue
          Larkspur, CA 94939

Thank you for your order.
E-Mail JJILKB@aol.com